I0460542

Arizona Free

Doug Martin

Kanspira Publishing

Los Angeles - Kansas City

ISBN: 978-0-9844500-0-8

Library of Congress Control Number: 2010903534

www.kanspira.com

Contents

1

GasMax

"I just don't know if this is right" Jason said, as he and Tony sat motionless in the Jeep Wrangler at the travel plaza on the western end of Phoenix. A herd of vehicles lay congregated before them on the gas station plains like nervous wildebeests sipping a wary drink of water. It was a beautiful day outside and the fresh air was palpable; Tony could feel his animalistic inner salesperson starting to get all worked up, and imagined himself as a hungry lion waiting to pounce. And yet Jason had always had more of a conscience than his zealous friend. The idea of cornering innocent travelers as they filled up their gas tanks in order to pester them with a canned sales pitch had predictably induced an uneasy feeling in him and kept him from opening the Wrangler's door.

"If what's right?" Tony asked.

It was an obscure product, and one that Jason wasn't even sure that people actually needed. Though pressured by his eager friend, he felt comfortable in his questioning skepticism nonetheless. Wasn't it, after all, the moral imperative of the salesperson, he reasoned, to believe in one's own product before strong arming others into buying it? He had seen the infomercials and its claims were impressive: improved gas mileage; saving money, the environment, and ultimately the planet. And yet he'd never even tried a single can of GasMax before, so there was no way of knowing if the claims were true.

"Well, I mean, we're not supposed to be soliciting people at their cars while they're filling up" Jason said. "I mean, how would you like it if someone came up to you while you were pumping gas and tried to sell you something?"

The question came off sounding a bit confrontational but was really an attempt to eliminate any doubt in his own mind about his purpose here. He wanted to sell GasMax. He needed the money. He just wasn't sure about the approach his friend has chosen.

"How else are we supposed to sell this stuff then, Jason? We have to at least go out there and try!" Tony urged.

"Yea, but you said it pretty much sells itself, didn't you?"

"Well not literally it doesn't! We still have to tell people about it. So are you in or out?" Tony asked, opening the door. Jason hesitated.

"Come on Jason," Tony said, making one last pitch to convince his wavering friend, "this is the opportunity we've been looking for, man! And just look at all these people..." he said, broadly surveying the landscape of the travel plaza, rich with gas guzzling cars and trucks. The possibilities seemed endless. "This is the right place to do it! We got heavy traffic here, lots of gas pumps. Must be a hundred people an hour passing through here! And just think..." he said, thumbing to the case of GasMax in the back seat, "we only need to sell ten of these little cans an hour... that's it! Just ten an hour and we're golden! That's a hundred bucks an hour, fifty bucks each, split 50/50. That's way more than we make at MOSH!"

His persistence chipped away at Jason's resolve.

"Alright, fine Tony. Ten per hour and you're right... that's a lot more than we're making now. Just one thing though, how much did these things cost you?"

Tony had to think for a moment.

"Uh, I paid like about $250 for all of 'em, I think."

"$250?!" Jason asked incredulously. "So then you mean we're really only making about five bucks on each can then?"

"Um, about five bucks, yeah that sounds about right" Tony replied.

"So then that's about *half* what we thought we were making. How are we going to be able to quit our jobs on *that*?"

"Twenty-five bucks an hour each, are you kidding me? We can tell MOSH to go shove it for twenty-five bucks an hour! And think about it: no more alarm clock, no more bosses. We can be our own bosses!" Tony said, dredging up the desperate mantra of the entrepreneur dreamer; the freedom from shackles of financial servitude, which when brought to its full fruition would inevitably result in carefree frolic with bountiful, wind-swept haired babes amongst endless green hills alive with the sound of music: the mind-numbing norm of those who had put in the hard work and were now reaping their just rewards.

"That's great Tony, but we'll only make twenty-five an hour if we stick it out here for a full five hours and sell *ten* of them each hour. What if we don't sell *any* of them?"

"What if we sell a hundred of them?" Tony retorted quickly with a challenge of his own.

"We don't even *have* a hundred of them! We only have those ones you bought off that ad," Jason said.

"We can order more" Tony replied, so sure of himself and his plan. Jason fell silent for a few moments but finally capitulated, half out of hoping that the plan would actually work, and half out of proving to his friend that he had once again underestimated the difficulty of reaching those endless green hills.

"Alright, fine. Worst case, you're stuck with fifty cans of GasMax and you eat 250 bucks."

"Best case we make 500 bucks today."

"Alright then it's settled, so let's do this" Jason said, at last opening the door.

The two friends got out of the Jeep and stood tall with renewed confidence. For Jason, the matter had been decided at last. He would give his friend's latest scheme a chance to work. After all, they had often talked at work about all of the things they could be doing to break out of the corporate rut, but had never actually acted on any of them. This time was different though. Tony finally made the first move and purchased the inventory. From there the gears were turning and there was no stopping them until they found either smashing success or abysmal failure. It was a simple matter of selling the inventory now that would determine their destiny, Jason reasoned. The Fates would be weaving their destiny through the hands of those noble travelers filling up their vehicles at the gas pumps less than a hundred yards away from them.

They decided to split up and work separately. It seemed harmless enough to approach a potential prospect that way; a person could easily feel intimidated by two strangers accosting them at once. Jason scanned the parking lot and eyed a potential new client filling up her tank.

It was a middle-aged woman driving a minivan, probably somewhere in between kid delivery and pick-up. As he approached her, she pretended not to notice. But she became increasingly agitated as Jason drew nearer. He had the entire parking lot to himself to walk around in, and yet was coming right at her in what was soon becoming an obvious trajectory. He rehearsed the lines under his breath that Tony had given him as motivation, promising him that they would work: 'people *need* this product! I'm doing them a favor! I care a lot about people, that's why I want them to save money and to save our planet by helping my clients get better gas mileage…'

As he approached to within ten feet of the woman she quickly snatched her printed receipt and opened the van door.

"Excuse me," Jason said, hurrying to catch her, ready to unload his sales pitch. "Excuse me!"

But she had already closed the door and started the engine. She smiled nervously at Jason and threw it in Drive, speeding away and leaving him standing there in disbelief. He didn't even get a chance to say Hello.

The thought crossed his mind, *what if I was a secret millionaire and I wanted to give you – a total stranger – a huge chunk of money? You wouldn't have gotten it from* me. *Bitch.*

Tony was on the opposite side of the island and was having no better luck with his first prospect.

"Do the owners know you're out here?" an old man asked him sharply.

"Yes sir, yes they do" Tony fibbed. "And they highly recommend GasMax. You see, they care about saving money for their customers, and this product is just the ticket to-"

"Bah!" the old man shouted and waved Tony away with a flick of his hand. "Fluff!" he said, then drove off, shaking his head to make his point.

Jason could see that his friend was handed his first rejection, but seemed to be taking it like a champ.

"Rough start!" he yelled over to Tony.

"Yea, but give it a minute, it'll turn around!" his eternally optimistic friend replied. "Live for the 'No' Jason, because it means you're that much closer to the 'Yes'!"

He could always count on Tony to keep a fresh supply of salesman bullshit in stock. But he admired that about his friend, knowing that navigating through life required plenty of never-give-up.

The two friends worked the travel plaza for three hours and didn't sell a single can of GasMax. Jason had gotten as far in his spiel as mentioning the price, but was promptly laughed at when he told them 'ten dollars'.

"Other stores sell that stuff for five bucks!" a man told him.

"No, I'm sorry, but that's incorrect sir" Jason replied, quickly pivoting to one of his 'overcoming objections' scripts. "You see, GasMax is not sold in any stores. It's a-"

"There's a reason for that!" the man said, turning his back on him.

"Yes sir, yes there is. And the reason is because it's a uniquely formulated blend of-"

"'Gas Release' is what you ought to call it... as in the stuff that's coming out of your butt crack! It'll ruin your engine, too!" the man added for good measure.

"No sir, it does not ruin anyone's engine."

"Did you know that stuff clogs up your car's valves like cholesterol? Eventually your car will have a heart attack if you're not careful. No Thank You!" the man said as he got inside his car and left.

"I'm going to have a heart attack..." Jason said quietly to himself.

Unsure of what to do next, he scanned the pumps to find Tony, who was just finishing up with his latest rejection, living for the 'no' as if it were his last day on Earth. There was only one customer left in the entire travel center. Apparently they had scared the rest of the herd away. But it only took one wildebeest, and this one looked promising. It was a very frail elderly woman standing next to her old Buick. Jason headed over her way before Tony could spot her. She didn't even see him coming and he knew she couldn't go far.

"Uh, excuse me, ma'am?" Jason politely asked.

The old woman took a few seconds to turn herself around towards the voice she was sure she was hearing.

"Yes sonny?" she asked through thick coke bottle glasses.

He had her right where he wanted her. She was not fast enough to escape.

"Yes ma'am. You see, the reason I came over here is because I noticed you're driving quite an old vehicle there, and I was wondering, how would you like to take your gas mileage up to the max?"

"Oh my… the max?"

"That's right ma'am," he said as he held up a can of GasMax. "Believe it or not, this little can right here can improve your fuel efficiency by over 20%! That's like going from twenty miles per gallon to over twenty-four miles per gallon! Or to put it another way, it's like getting five gallons of gas but only paying for four!"

"Really? That little can?"

This was going too well, Jason thought. There had to be a catch. Perhaps she was a plant. Tony's grandma? He could see Tony pumping his fist, encouraging him to close the sale.

"I'm not making it up, ma'am" Jason continued. "Now think about how much good you'd be doing for the environment by saving all that gas. Think about how much money you're saving. Let me ask you, do you have grandkids, ma'am?"

"Yes… last time I checked."

"Wonderful! Think about all that money you could be saving for them! You see, when you buy GasMax, you're really saying that you care about your grandkids. You do love your grandkids, don't you ma'am?"

That induced another fist pump from Tony. Jason was starting to feel slimy. It was the first time he used the 'you *do* love your family, don't you?' script. Tony highly recommended it. But something just didn't seem right about manipulating a poor old woman for her money, which had to be scarce enough already. He began feeling like one of those people who preys on the social security checks of the confused elderly. But with Tony watching, he knew he had to carry through with the deed.

"Yes, I suppose I do love my grandkids…" the old lady replied.

"Perfect, then it's a deal! A small ten dollar gift to show you love your grandkids is all it takes, and you can have this magic little can."

It was ugly but it worked. He managed to get her ten bucks and she couldn't have been any happier. Jason couldn't have felt any lower.

"You did her a big favor" Tony said afterwards.

2 ⊞

Encanto Park

"Okay, so it wasn't the best idea ever" Tony admitted as they sat in their cubicles at work the next day. "But we did manage to at least sell one can."

"*I* sold one. You didn't sell any" Jason replied.

"Okay, but the point is we did it together as a *team*, and we showed that it could work" Tony insisted.

"I'll give you that much, we did it together. But as far as I'm concerned the only thing that worked about it was that we proved you can still hoodwink old ladies in the 21st century."

"Hey hey hey, easy now," Tony said. "She seemed like a very intelligent person to me. Hell, she mighta been smarter than all of us here put together!"

A giggling voice came from over the cubicle wall. "Well that isn't hard to do!" It was Alice, the Scheduling group's admin. She giggled some more at her little joke and asked "You boys need me to order anything? Envelopes? Pens? Paperclips? I'm doing my office supplies shopping today."

"No, I'm good Alice" Jason replied.

"No thank you" Tony said.

"Alright then," Alice said. "Hey listen, can you two do me a *huge* favor while I'm gone? Can you keep an eye on my candy jars and just make sure no one takes any of them? My mint jar's been missing since yesterday and no one even bothered to bring it back."

Jason tipped a finger towards her. "We'll guard it with our lives."

"Oh, you silly boys!" she tittered, not perfectly in balance, but harmless nonetheless. The two young men always brought a smile to her face.

"Hey" Tony said as she left.

"Yea" Jason answered, finishing up an email.

"Did I tell you what my cousin's been doing?"

"No."

"He's flipping houses. And get this: he's already done about a dozen of 'em so far and he's made like about $50,000 doing it."

"That's it?"

"What do you mean 'that's it', that's a lot of money!"

"Not for twelve houses, it isn't! Do you know how long it takes and how much work goes into doing just *one* of those deals? It's not like what you see on TV. It'll kill you. Or ruin your marriage. Or make you go broke," Jason said.

"And how is it that you know all about this and are such an expert all of a sudden?" Tony asked.

"My mom knows somebody who's done it before, back home in Topeka. They said never again. Plus you gotta time the market just right or else you'll be stuck in it."

"No you don't, that's the nice part about it! Doesn't matter what the market's doing!"

"Really? That's not what he said."

"Well, so… you're gonna let *one* guy you know who wasn't that great at it ruin your whole impression of it?

That's a sure way to shut the door to opportunity, my friend."

"I'm not saying *you* can't do it. Go right ahead."

"Maybe I will!" Tony said defiantly.

"Good."

"Soon as I get some start-up capital" he said, noticing Cynthia from Purchasing walking past the cubicle wall.

"Psst… Jason!" he whispered excitedly.

"What?"

"Take a look at this" he said, pointing discreetly towards the wall. "Isn't that the new girl you've been talking about? The one that plays tennis?"

Jason rose from his chair and peered out carefully over the wall, as if eyeing an enemy fortification.

"Yea, that's her. Wow, she looks nice today."

"Yes she does. Oh, and I meant to tell you… I found out where she plays tennis at."

"You did? How'd you find that out?"

"Oh, Larry over in Commodities knows her. Said she plays every Saturday morning at Encanto Park… 8AM. We should go there someday and you know… run into her."

"Run into her?" Jason said. "We can't just show up there!"

"Why not?"

"Well, because it would look too weird. And besides, I don't play tennis. That's a gay sport. She'd think I was on a date with you or something."

"Oh my God, the things you come up with just because you're afraid to meet her!"

"I'm not afraid," Jason replied. "I'm not afraid of anything."

"Uh huh, sure. Okay Encanto Park it is then, bright and early this Saturday morning."

"Never."

᛭᛭᛭

"Wow, you look really gay" Tony said to Jason, who was dressed in tennis whites, complete with white tennis shoes and white socks that went halfway up his leg.

"Shut up, you don't look all that cool yourself... like the missing member from Kajagoogoo or something."

Tony threw his hands up in the air. "Seriously, only you would even know they *had* a missing member. It's the Andre Agassi look from the '80s, okay? So are you ready?"

"Let's see... it's 8:45 on a Saturday morning. I should be in bed right now and I have no idea how to play tennis. Of course I'm ready. Let's go."

"You got a racquet?" Tony asked.

"Right here," he said, picking up an old wooden Wilson racquet, circa 1983, from a table stand near the door. "Got this in a garage sale a long time ago. But more importantly, I have balls" he said, flashing a can of Penns.

"We'll see about that" Tony answered.

They left Jason's apartment and drove to Encanto Park. It was a nice park, with walking trails, a lake, and several tennis courts. It was a well-kept place, with nice landscaping, and of course a large sign out front, 'Encanto Park'.

"Oh man, what am I doing here?" Jason asked rhetorically, putting his head in his hands. "She's gonna think I suck."

"No, she's gonna *know* you suck. You don't know how to play, right?"

"Do I *look* like I know how to play? Of course I don't know how to play, are you kidding me! I think I played maybe once when I was a kid. That was probably when my parents decided to put me into little league."

"That turned out well" Tony said.

"It turned out just fine, thank you" Jason replied. "I'm just a little nervous right now, that's all."

They parked and got ready to disembark.

"Okay now, remember…" Jason said. "This needs to look like a coincidence that we're here. I can't have her thinking I'm stalking her or anything."

"You got it buddy" Tony said. "We'll just walk right over there and act surprised as hell when we see her."

Jason pointed a confirming finger, tapping it in the air because his friend was on to something. "Surprised as hell, I like that."

They gathered their racquets and balls and made their way over to the courts. There were eight of them in all and every one of them was empty except for one. As they walked closer they could tell it was Cynthia playing on Court 1 with one of her friends.

"It's her!" Tony whispered excitedly.

"Yea, but what are we gonna do? We can't just play right next to them, that'll look too creepy."

"Let's take this court over here" Tony said. "It's not next to her, but it's close enough."

"Okay, sounds good" Jason agreed. They opened the gate to the court, feeling a bit out of place, and walked over to the bench near the net as Cynthia and her friend played a long rally.

"Wow, they're good!" Jason said, watching the two of them hit back and forth. They hit several powerful shots to each other, until Cynthia finally flubbed one into the net. She looked over at Jason and Tony and waved politely, seeming confused about what they were doing there.

"Oh, hey Cynthia!" Tony called out and waved at her, a bit too desperately for Jason's liking. "I'm surprised to see you here!"

"Why? We play here every Saturday morning. I'm surprised to see the two of you here."

Tony forced a laugh. "Everyone's surprised!"

"Don't be a dork!" Jason whispered to him. "Hi Cynthia!"

They didn't know her friend, but she was just as Anna Kournikova-ish as Cynthia.

"Yea, we just thought we'd shake off the cobwebs a little," Tony said with false bravado, going into some kind of bizarre stretching routine with his upper torso, "you know, get the rust out."

"I see…" she said.

"Okay that's enough" Jason whispered.

There was a brief delay, but it seemed like minutes to Jason because of the awkward silence. Then Cynthia and her friend went back to rallying as if the two of them weren't even there.

Not entirely sure of what to do next, they began doing stretching exercises and jogging in place to warm up. Jason felt even sorrier than ever before that he had agreed to Tony's idea. He could see Cynthia and her friend occasionally glancing over at them, probably curious about how good they must be in order to require so much warm up time, pulling their arms over their heads, tilting to the side, and bending their legs and knees this way and that. Jason dreaded the start of their playing like he dreaded death itself.

"Let's hit close to the net first, we can't miss too badly that way" he suggested.

"Okay" Tony agreed, and the two of them stood on opposite sides of the net, no more than ten feet away from each other.

"Just hit it to me. Not hard though" Jason whispered, trying to look over at Cynthia to see if she was watching, without appearing too obvious. To him it seemed as if his every move was being recorded and analyzed, and a panic struck him briefly: what if they had one of those tiny camcorders and they actually *were* recording him in between shots? He felt sure that he would have frozen up, if it weren't for the fact that he and Tony hadn't even started yet.

Tony got the party started. He tapped the ball softly and it went to Jason's backhand. Jason swung and missed. He wanted to disappear.

"Okay, no problem. Here's another one," Tony said, tapping another one over the net. This time Jason made contact, but whacked it too hard and the ball went flying off the court.

"Don't worry about it, the fence stopped it" Tony said.

"Here let me serve, maybe I'll do better," Jason suggested. He pulled a ball out from his pocket and tapped it toward Tony. Tony hit it back to Jason, but Jason swung and missed it again.

"How'd you get so good?" Jason asked his friend.

Tony shrugged his shoulders. "I don't know, I guess I watched some of it on TV."

"And that actually works?"

"Sure it does. Anytime you can get your brain to imagine making your body do something, you'll do much better at it. It's called 'visualization' Jason. They use it in some sales programs. You should try it sometime. You know, 'visualize' success and it makes it that much more likely that it's going to happen."

"Visualization, huh?"

"Yea."

"As in, if I can just visualize Cynthia wanting to go out with me, then it'll happen?"

"Well, yea…" Tony replied. "But you also have to work for it. You can't just rely on wishful thinking alone."

"You got a point there," Jason said. "Come on, let's get a drink. I'm thirsty already."

They walked over to their bags on the bench and Jason pulled out his jug of water. He might have visualized earlier that he would be chugging it after three hours of vigorous exercise – dumping it over his head and letting the flowing wetness cool him – but it was pretty obvious that that wasn't going to be happening. Not today at least.

"You think they're gonna play much longer?" Jason asked, keeping an eye on them.

"I don't know. You might want to make your move before it's too late."

"Make my move? What's my move supposed to be?"

"I don't know. Should we just ask them to play some doubles with us?"

"Oh, god no," Jason said. "That would be a disaster." He could see Cynthia looking over his way and smiling. It appeared that she and her friend were laughing about something.

"Maybe I should just go over there and talk to her?" he said, beginning to formulate a bold plan.

"Well… that would be the ballsy thing to do" his friend agreed.

"Yea, it would huh. Okay, I'll do it."

Jason put the water bottle down on the bench and walked over to the two girls. Tony stayed behind, amazed that his friend was actually going to do something instead of just talk about it.

"Hi Cynthia" Jason said, trying to sound as masculine and self-assured as he could possibly muster.

"Oh, hi Jason" Cynthia quickly said between shots without looking at him. She and her friend just kept playing. It was too awkward to leave it at just that, so he knew he had to think of something else to stimulate the conversation a little more.

"Say… you two are really, really good! I'm impressed!" He knew it sounded dorky, but it was the best he could think of at the moment.

Cynthia made another unforced error and stopped hitting for a moment. She turned to address Jason.

"Listen, my friend and I are really busy right now. We're getting ready for a tournament. I'd love to stop and chat with you, but time just won't allow for that. But it was really nice to see both of you." Her last sentence was said in a conclusive manner, as if to say 'I'm done with you now', and she continued hitting.

"Okay… sorry to bother you then…" he said, beginning his retreat. "Good luck in the tournament!"

There was no response and he quickly walked back towards Tony. His friend could barely contain his excitement.

"What did she say?"

"Well, she was a little bitchy. But it looks like we need to start playing tournaments. It's the only way."

3

Opportunities

It was Sunday morning and Jason had planned on sleeping in, but the phone woke him up much too soon.

"Hello?" he answered groggily.

"Jason? Is that you?" Tony asked.

"I don't know. Where am I?"

"It sounds like you're in bed probably."

"Oh yea, because it's kind of early…"

"I know but listen, I got it!" Tony said.

"You got it?"

"Yea!"

"You got what?"

"I got the business opportunity we've been looking for to really get ahead this time!"

"What, more GasMax?"

"No, something different."

"But did you have to tell me right now? Couldn't this wait?"

"It probably could have, but listen, 'cuz I'm driving right now and I'm really excited about it!"

"I can tell."

"It's domain names, Jason!"

"What?"

"Domain names! You know, like whazzawhazza.com, spielenfoolen.com, chittychottychangaroo.com?"

"Huh?"

"They're domain names. And I bought them! They're mine now!"

"Yea… and?"

"And… so the idea is you buy all these great domain names and then you sell them on the aftermarket to people who are willing to pay a *pretty hefty* premium for really creative domain names like that."

"They are?"

"Oh yea Jason, and think about it: no inventory, no overhead. Very little upfront investment to get started!"

"But who'd want to pay a lot of money for some stupid domain names like that?"

"Stupid names, are you kidding me? These are creative names, Jason! And that's where the value comes in: we bring the creativity. And they pay for it!"

"Have you actually sold any of them yet? And what's that loud music in the background?"

"It's my Rush CD… it's a song called 'Dreamline'. And no, I haven't sold any yet, but I just got started, give me a break."

"It's probably because people don't want to pay a lot of money for something that they can just make up by themselves. I think you need more useful names."

"Oh yea, like what?" Tony asked.

"You know, 'besthotels.com',

'grandmascookies.com', 'localjobs.com'. Places where people might actually want to go. No one's gonna go to those websites you just mentioned and set up actual businesses with them."

"Oh really? And do the names Yahoo or Google ring any bells with you?"

"Yes of course, but they had real business plans, which, I'm guessing, you probably don't."

"Not yet, but I'm working on it. That's why I need your help!"

"If you're looking to me for a business plan then you're sniffing up the wrong tree my friend. MBA ubergenius I am not."

"Hmm, okay. Well I'll let you know how it goes. But if I call you up one day and say 'hey guess what, I'm a millionaire', then don't be too surprised."

"Because someone bought huzzahuzza from you."

"Right."

"Okay Tony, I'll try not to act too surprised."

"Hey anyway, listen. We need to head over to Hooters this afternoon. Hope you didn't have any plans."

╬╬╬

"Hey boys, come on over and have a seat!" Phil said loudly. "I was just having a drink and talking to my friends over here!"

They had known Phil through work for a couple of years now, but he was more like Tony's friend than Jason's. He was a workhorse of a drinker at Hooters, an obnoxious fixture with his own line item on the P&L. But even rowdy drunks were sometimes full of cash, and it was often easier

to separate them from their money. Phil was no exception.
The waitresses obligingly feigned their worship of the porky
patron, a form of acting that resulted in getting paid quite
nicely when done correctly.

They sat down at Phil's table.

"You remember my friends Tony and Jason, right?"
Phil asked Bedroom Eyes.

"No, I don't think we've met before" she smiled
with big beautiful bulbous blue eyes.

Jason hadn't started drinking yet, but he had the
distinct feeling that her penetrating gaze was not meant
solely for theater. "Glad that we're meeting now" he said.

"Come on," Sharon Kisses said to Bedroom Eyes.
"We better get going before Charlie gets mad again."

They quickly took the newcomers' drink orders and
then left.

"Ah, to Hell with Charlie, let him get angry!" Phil
bellowed, obviously way over-the-top-drunk again. "And
no more of that TSS garbage! Totally Shitty Stuff is what
they oughta call it!" His focus returned somewhat back to
his two friends as he shook his head in deep thought. "I trip
out on that stuff" he said.

Jason drank it all the time and never had a problem.
It seemed as if Phil was offering another flimsy excuse for
his excesses. Tony could see right through it as well.

"Seriously Phil…" Tony said, "how long have you
been here?"

"Oh, only an hour or so, boys. Oh, and hey by the
way, if she's Sharon Kisses then I'm Abel Johnson, if you
know what I'm talking about!" he laughed disgustingly.

"We know what you're talking about" Jason said
flatly, hoping his drink would come soon so he could
tolerate Phil's antics a little easier. And so he could see

Bedroom Eyes again. Their first encounter had been so shortly sweet.

Phil was quick with a subtle excuse for his alcoholic binging. "Yea, I've had just a couple of drinks is all, waiting on you guys to get here…"

"Yea, sorry we're late" Tony said. "Jason's tongue got stuck on a frozen forecast and we had to pull it off."

"Ouch! Hey no worries, it happens to the best of us!" Phil replied. "Besides, it's not like I just sat here with nothing to do! There's nice views! Good drinks. And this really far out show was on about meteors hitting the Earth or some weird shit like that and it caught my attention for a while." Poor show, Jason thought as Phil continued his rambling. "It was like… okay, so one minute everything's going great and then the next thing you know the scientists are telling everybody 'oh hey by the way there's this giant fucking rock out in space somewhere that's like the size of the *friggin' Himalayas* that's gonna crash into us and there's *nothing* we can do about it and we're all gonna *die* in six months when it wipes us all out!'"

"No shit?" Tony asked.

"Yea, no shit" Phil replied soberly. "Don't bother making funeral arrangements if it happens boys," he informed them, "'cuz nobody's gonna be at the funeral anyway, we're all gonna be cooked to a nice brown crisp like KFC! Speaking of that, Jesus am I getting hungry."

"Can't they just blast it with a nuke or something?" Jason asked, involving himself in the conversation as a means of passing the drinkless time more efficiently.

"They could, but they said it would just break up into like a *thousand* smaller rocks with the same effect. Basically we're just fucked either way."

"Yea, that doesn't give us a lot of options."

"Drinks are here!" Sharon Kisses said, handing

Tony and Jason their orders.

"Oh thank God. You're an angel" Tony said.

Sharon laughed. "So what have you boys been up to?"

"Oh, just talking about the end of all life on Earth as we know it" Jason said.

"Sounds exciting! Well, you know what they say: eat, drink, and be merry, for tomorrow you may die."

"Ain't that the truth" Jason said.

Sharon laughed as she went about her way – a good humored disposition that was somewhat inappropriate for the subject matter at hand, yet certainly not atypical for such a place as steeped in substance as Hooters.

"You know," Tony said as if to enlighten, 'they say all those meteors brought water and life to the Earth."

"Really?" Phil asked.

"Yea, you know, a lot of those things have water ice on them" Tony said. "They probably made the oceans a long time ago even, when the Earth was being bombarded by millions of meteors."

"And life too?" Phil asked.

"Yea well, they say they have the basic building blocks of life in them already. And when they finally had the right conditions here on Earth, boom! Life."

"Boom? No shit? Just like that?" Phil asked.

"Well , I mean I don't know how *long* it took to happen. I wasn't there. But that's the scenario anyway" Tony replied.

Phil nudged Jason jokingly on the elbow. "Sounds like someone paid attention in science class, eh Jason?"

"Tony's a very smart guy" he replied matter-of-factly between pulls on the bottle.

"I had an astrobiology class in college" Tony said.

"No shit?" Phil asked.

"Yea, I'm totally serious. We learned about DNA and hydrothermal vents and Drake's equation and everything else. It was really cool."

"I bet" Phil said. "And I'll tell you something else that's pretty cool, speaking of DNA. I'm meeting with a guy tomorrow to talk about this great new product opportunity that's supposed to be sweeping the planet. I'll tell you more about it a little later Tony."

"New product?" Tony asked.

"Yea. And speaking of blowing things up like asteroids, let's just say it's like dynamite!"

4 ╫╫╫╫

DiNAmite

"Umm… no, I don't believe we've met" Cynthia said hesitantly as she was introduced to Cloe at the company's annual picnic. She didn't know her personally, but like everyone else who worked at Murman Outdoor Supply House, she knew *of* her. Cloe was a nice enough person and was well-liked by most, yet she tended to live on the eccentric edge, which sometimes caused others to keep their distance from her as a guarded precaution against the unknown.

"That's because you're in Purchasing, and I'm in Scheduling!" Cloe said brightly. She was nothing if not cheery.

"So we are…" Cynthia replied, withdrawing her hand; a bizarre expression on her face completely unhidden. She often evoked that kind of response in others, the girl with the four letter name. Too cheery for most, her positivity was off-center to the unusual figure she struck: a skinny girl pale in complexion, rose tattoos on her forearms, and silver jewelry abundantly shimmering across her form like a modern Caucasian pharaoh; large silver earrings, silver bracelets, silver necklaces, and even a tiny silver ornament pinned to one of her nostrils. She didn't wear make-up – had no use for it – and kept her hair short and purple, for low maintenance and her favorite color. She was comfortable in her skin and wasn't trying to hide anything from anyone, with a surprising natural beauty whose power was transformative enough to outshine even her somewhat dour, almost gothic-like exterior. Even though she had the natural beauty, her downfall – and the reason that Jason, the object of her pursuit didn't pursue her back – was that she could be spastic at times, so much so that those who didn't avoid her due to her exploding cheeriness usually fell into the other group: those who avoided her because she was an old-school spaz. Jason fell into the latter camp, and even coined a nickname for her: "gork", which was short for a girl dork. Tony on the other hand didn't mind her one bit and found her to be a fun person to hang out with, gorky and all. But then, Tony was not pursuing any one particular girl at the moment that he just had to have. That was Jason's illness.

"Well, it certainly was nice meeting you," Cynthia said to Cloe, ready to move on and get away from the Scheduling nerds. She found them to be less glamorous than Purchasing. And besides, the Purchasing tribe had set up camp around the volleyball net, and Cynthia was in the mood to show off a little of her bump-set-spike.

"Oh the pleasure was all mine!" Cloe gleefully exclaimed. "Hey wait a minute! Before you go…you see that guy over there… Jason Newcastle?" She pointed to Jason, who was standing next to Tony as they watched the annual one-legged ass-kicking contest.

"Yes, of course I see him. What about him?" Cynthia asked somewhat impatiently.

"Well… I saw you talking to him the other day. What's your secret?"

"What do you mean? There's no secret" Cynthia said. "I mean, he came up to me and asked me if I knew of any good sushi restaurants in the area. He's such a nerd though. He doesn't even know how to play tennis."

"Really?" Cloe asked. "Because I've been trying to get him to ask me out on a date for a long time now!"

"Oh, well then why don't you just skip the courting bullshit and ask *him* out on a date? It's a new millennium, Cl…" she struggled to remember the name.

"Cloe."

"Cloe… right. It's a new millennium Cloe. Girls ask guys out on dates all the time."

"They do?"

"Of course they do! Just go over there and say hello and ask him! Come on, they're not that hard to figure out. Guys are *sooo* easy. They'd practically *beg* a girl to ask them out! You have nothing to lose. All he can do is say no."

"That's the part I'm afraid of."

"Well don't be. I guarantee you he'll say yes. Now I gotta get going, they're waiting for me over at volleyball. Good luck Cl…"

"Cloe."

"Right. Good luck!"

"Thanks…"

Pondering it some more, she began to think that perhaps Cynthia was right. Maybe it was just as easy as saying the words, *will you… with me?* Her courage summoned, she took a deep breath and walked over to where Jason was standing. But her spastic element got the better of her and she tripped on a rock ten feet in front of him, face-planting herself into the dirt.

Jason and Tony rushed over to make sure she was alright.

"Are you okay?" Jason asked. "You took a pretty bad fall there!"

She looked up from the dirt and blew a grass blade

from her lips.

"Want to get sushi sometime?" she asked him.

Jason stared at her for a couple of seconds before bursting out in laughter.

"That's my pickup line!"

"I know" Cloe said. "Cynthia told me about it."

"She did? Are you good friends with her or something?" Jason asked.

"No, I just met her today. But she said you asked her out for sushi. That's how I knew you liked sushi."

"Actually, I don't even like sushi" Jason replied. "I was just asking her because I knew *she* did."

"Wait…" Tony interjected, confused. "Who likes sushi here?"

"None of us, apparently" Jason said.

"How about a steak?" Cloe asked, smiling. "Mmmm… steak."

"Listen, Cloe…" Jason began. "You're a really cool girl and all… but honestly… well, I'm more into the Cynthia type" he said, in what he believed to be a tactful manner. There was never an easy let-down.

"You are, huh…" Cloe said, dejected and not her usual cheery self.

"Yea… and I'm sorry to break it to you, but it's best to be upfront with people, ya know."

Tony interrupted.

"I'll go out with you, Cloe… for sushi… or steak… or anything else."

"You will?" Cloe asked.

"Sure!"

"Okay, that sounds good!"

"I'll call you to set it up then" Tony said.

"Okay, that sounds good!" Cloe said, standing up, brushing herself off, and smiling as she left.

Jason looked at Tony, surprised. "That sounds good?"

"I haven't told you about this yet" Tony said. "But there's this great new product I want to introduce you to. But first I need to test out my sales pitch on some other people. She'll be perfect for that."

"Another new product idea?" Jason asked.

"I know, I know. But trust me, this one's good."

"Why wouldn't I trust you?"

⚏⚏⚏

"How'd your date with the Gork go last night?" Jason asked as they ate their lunch at Pizza Queen. Tony had heard that they were getting rid of their all-you-can-eat buffet and wanted to take advantage of it before the place modernized and started charging more for less.

"It wasn't a date" Tony replied. "Cloe and I just went out for sushi, that's all."

"Uh huh… just sushi."

"So what if it *was* a date anyway, why do you care?"

"I don't care" Jason replied.

"You sound a little jealous to me."

"I'm not jealous. I think Cloe's cool, she's just a little too weird for me, that's all."

"Ahh…" Tony feigned sympathy. "What's the

matter, Cynthia hasn't called? Face it champ, you're just not good enough for her. She wants someone with ball control. And you just don't have that, on any level."

"Well I'm not giving up. I'll find a way to get her to notice me. I'm taking up tennis lessons, you know."

"Dude you are not gonna take up tennis lessons, stop kidding yourself. And even if you *did* it's not like you'd be any good anytime soon! It takes *years* to be able to play like her! She looked semi-pro!"

"I'll practice three hours a day if I have to. I'll get up early and hit the courts at 4am if that's what it takes. Would you join me if I did? It could be like we're in the military."

"You're such a wanna-be, Jason. Getting up early is not my thing. Not for tennis anyway, once was enough."

Jason seemed dejected. "Yea, you're probably right, tennis isn't my thing. I might never get her attention. I don't know how I possibly could, at least not without getting promoted at MOSH a few times in rapid succession."

Tony thought he had the answer. "There is one way…" he began, "if you're willing to do just like I'm doing with Cloe…"

"What are you doing with Cloe?"

"See… it's what I've been talking about Jason, you can't just look at it as if you're going out with her on some kind of a 'date'. Instead, just look at it as if it's a chance to show her something."

"I'm not following here" Jason said, "what exactly would I be showing her?"

"Well, what you'd be showing her is this great new product that I'm selling right now, just like I showed it to Cloe last night!"

"Oh, I see. Yea… how'd that go by the way?"

"Like magic! She's buying three cases from me already!"

"Three cases? You're shittin' me."

"I'm not shittin' you" Tony replied.

"Okay, then what is this stuff?"

"It's called 'DiNAmite', my friend. It's a new energy drink that's the most incredible product ever!"

"Dynamite?"

"No, 'DiNAmite'. As in it contains real dinosaur DNA that's supposed to give you all this incredible strength and energy."

"Dinosaur DNA? Now you're talking crazy."

"I can explain more to you tonight Jason, but just listen, it works."

"Hmm… I don't know."

"Look, would I have sold three cases to Cloe if it didn't work?"

"I don't know. I mean, how would *she* know whether it works or not?"

"Because I let her try some! She was hooked on it right away!"

"Yea but that's Cloe for you. Who knows the kinds of things she gets herself hooked on" Jason said.

"Just trust me brother. Will you go with me tonight to a meeting with some of my uplines?"

"Uplines? Oh God, you mean like in some kind of multi-level marketing scam?"

"No, it's not MLM, even though it looks and talks just like MLM. And don't worry, it's not a pyramid either. Yea, okay, so it costs money to join, you get paid to recruit others, and there's an eventual tipping point that leaves the masses at the bottom of the pyramid getting screwed while the founders inevitably bail out and create some new supposedly non-pyramidal scheme someplace else. But look, I'll explain everything later. So would you at least agree to go with me and keep an open mind about it?"

"Hmm…"

Tony needed to stop Jason's hesitation in its tracks. "This is the one, brother! I'm telling you… this is it! All those other things we tried are *bullshit* compared to this! Just give it a chance Jason! Don't let your dreams die, man…"

"Whatever. Alright fine, I'll go."

"Yes!"

"But only for 30 minutes or so… and I'm not buying anything!"

5 ⧠

Groupdrink

They arrived at the hotel on the outskirts of town. It was 7:00 and the event was about to get started.

"Why so far away from everything?" Jason asked as they got out of the Wrangler.

"I don't know" Tony answered. "Probably cheaper that way. Or maybe the conference rooms at the other places were all booked."

"Conference rooms? How many people are going to be at this thing?"

Tony shrugged his shoulders. "Who knows, could be hundreds. Could be thousands. It's a big deal, Jason. People come from all over the state for this. Kenny Graham's going to be here."

"Like I'm supposed to know who that is?"

"No, you wouldn't know him" Tony replied as they entered the hotel. "Phil told me all about him though. Kenny's huge in the organization. He's a Mega-Mega-Diamond."

"Sounds pretty damn important."

"He is."

"But not as important as a Mega-Mega-Mega Diamond, I bet" Jason said.

"There is no such thing" Tony answered. "Mega-Mega is as high as it goes. Anyway, it just means that he has a whole bunch of people under him… his downlines."

"Are you one of them?"

"Oh yea, you bet! You have to understand, this is like going to see the Pope, man! The guy's so rich he drives a different car every day of the week! He's worshipped by half the organization, I bet!"

"That's creepy" Jason replied. "You sure have learned a lot in such a small amount of time, Tony… a lot of creepy information."

"Yea well, Phil was pretty adamant that I learn as much as I could. He seems to be in love with Kenny. Or at least with his kind of lifestyle."

"Is he going to be here tonight?" Jason asked.

"Yes, he said he would. But he's helping get everything set up, so we might not see too much of him."

They approached an overcaffeinated guy in a suit who was playing doorman.

"Hey folks, how are we all doing?" the man said rapidly, with eyebrows turned up in far too much excitement than was warranted. "Are we all here to see Kenny G. this evening?"

"Kenny G.?" Jason asked.

"That's Kenny Graham, the Mega-Mega-Diamond" Tony said.

"The one and only!" the doorman added.

"Yes, we're here for Kenny" Tony confirmed.

"All of us…" Jason said.

"Great! Then that'll be $5 each for cover charge, please."

"Cover charge? For what?" Jason asked.

"Oh, you know, to help defray expenses. We had to rent this big room here," the man said quickly.

"Why doesn't Kenny just pay for it? It's his event. He makes enough money, doesn't he?" Jason said.

"Shhh!" Tony said and handed the doorman $10. "This is for both of us. Sorry about my friend, he's new. It's his first event."

"His first event? DiNAmite!" the dork said. "Go right on in! Kenny should be here any minute now!"

They walked into the conference room and found a couple of empty chairs. There was loud dance energy music playing, *Y'all Ready for This?* As if these people needed to get anymore worked up, Jason thought.

Tony recognized a face and from across the room. "There's Terry" he said, smiling and waving like familiar acquaintances. "He's a real nutcase. Still brags about how he caught one of Olivia Newton-John's leg warmers during the *Physical* tour. But he totally believes in the product, so he's pretty cool I guess. That's important to have, Jason: you gotta believe in what you're selling, or else people will see right through you."

"Do you believe in what you're selling?" Jason asked.

"Oh yea, totally! It's scientifically proven stuff. It has vitamins and minerals and all that, which are things that have been proven to be beneficial for your body. Or at least, they can't hurt, right? It's supposed to cure heart disease and cancer and stuff too. Plus it's got anti-oxidants to keep you from aging. It's really a miracle drink, is what it is."

"Fights cancer and heart disease too? How come I've never heard about this before?"

"I don't know for sure, but Phil thinks it's because

there's this big conspiracy by the doctors and the hospitals. See, they don't want you knowing about it, because then they'd go out of business if everyone started drinking this stuff."

"People would stop dying…"

"Well, I mean they wouldn't *stop* dying, but maybe they wouldn't die quite as often."

"You sound like a true believer to me, Tony. I think you'd do a great job selling it."

"Oh I am, totally! I trust my uplines, they told me all about it. They would never steer me wrong, believe me. One of the most important things you learn right away is, 'always trust your uplines'. Besides, I mean you can't get people to pay the prices they're paying for this stuff if they don't think it's valuable to them. Plus not to mention the dinosaur DNA which gives it the real kick. I didn't really elaborate very much on that to you earlier. You'll hear more about it from Kenny I'm sure, but that's what people are really paying for when they buy this stuff."

"And you believe all of this? You believe they actually found a way to… first of all *extract* the dinosaur DNA intact, notwithstanding all the technical challenges that would entail after millions of years, and the fact that all that *Jurassic Park* stuff is bullshit, and *then* to somehow mass-produce it and get FDA approval and everything else that would be required before people could, you know, start to actually put it into their bodies?"

"Uh huh. You gotta believe in it if you're gonna sell it, Jason. It's all about the 'mindset'."

"Okay, yea mindset, right, whatever. So that's why it's called 'DiNAmite', because it supposedly has dinosaur DNA in it. And it gives you energy. I get it."

"Exactly! See, I knew you'd get it right away Jason! When you explain it to people their eyes light up and it's like boom! You *know* they're getting it. That's the great thing about this product, it practically sells itself!"

"Is the DNA proven to be beneficial too?" Jason asked.

"Well, no one knows for sure" Tony replied. "But see, that's where the genius of marketing comes in. If you put that stuff in there – even just a little bit of it – then you'll get people thinking that it really is something unique and different – which it *is*, don't get me wrong – but I doubt the DNA has anything to do with the energy buzz. Sure, it has some vitamins and antioxidants and stuff, but the energy probably has a lot more to do with all the caffeine they put in there – like twelve cups' worth of coffee in one little can."

"Probably…" Jason said, looking around. It was intuitively obvious to even the most casual of observers that everyone in that room was hyped up on way too much of their own product, scurrying around like little agitated ants assessing the depth of the situation after some brat kid kicked dirt on them.

"Why didn't you invite Cloe to go?" Jason asked, as *We Like to Party* jammed out of the speakers. "This seems like the perfect crowd for her."

"I would have," Tony replied, "but I wasn't sure how she'd behave around you. She wouldn't be concentrating on the DiNAmite, she'd be thinking about the 'Jason might' the whole time. She'll come to the next one though, she already promised she would."

"Oh, that's fantastic" Jason said, doing his best not to step on Tony's vibe, which only seemed to be growing in intensity with each passing moment.

An announcer's voice broke over the loudspeaker. "Gooooood evening everybody!"

The colony of uplines and downlines broke into

another frenzy as it appeared closer to time for the event to start and Kenny Graham to make his much-anticipated appearance.

"How are we all doing out there tonight? Are we feeling *'DiNAmite'*?"

A fat man who might have passed for a baby brontosaurus startled Jason as he stood up and hollered, "DiNAmite every night!"

Scanning the crowd, Jason could see all eyes transfixed on the stage as if waiting for the Second Coming. The loudspeaker voice continued.

"It is my great pleasure to introduce to you a man who had a plan…"

"Amen!" someone in the crowd shouted.

"… a man who had a plan… and who took that plan five years ago and turned it into a reality…"

"Uh huh!"

"… and now today, five years later, that reality equals 3,000 downlines… and growing. Twelve million dollars worth of business… and growing. And now, ladies and gentlemen, I'm pleased to have you be among the first to hear the news… OUR NEW CEO… and growing!"

The crowd went wild.

"The new CEO! Oh my God!"

"No way! They promoted Kenny to CEO!"

Jason wasn't sure what to make of it all but he knew it had to be a big deal. Apparently the guy just got a big promotion.

"Now, ladies and gentlemen, please give a raucous *DiNAmite* welcome to our new CEO… Mister… Kenny… GRAHAM!"

The opening punches of the song 'Eye of the Tiger'

began playing and a man emerged from behind the curtain, shuffling his feet and throwing left jabs and right hooks, shadow boxing around stage to the roar of the delighted crowd.

"It's Kenny!" Tony shouted to Jason. "I've heard so much about him, but only seen him in pictures!"

The new CEO threw a quick combination of punches at an imaginary opponent to demonstrate he meant business. A real tough guy, Jason thought, built like a brickhouse, with a badass buzzcut to boot.

"Woooo! Yea! You want some of this?!" Kenny shouted to the crowd. "Do we have any *DiNAmite* salespeople out there in this audience tonight?"

"DiNAmite every night!" the chorus of converts shouted back on cue, as if reciting a well-rehearsed Hail Mary full of Grace.

"Well alright then!" Kenny shouted, smiling and attempting to catch his breath, as it appeared he had quickly knocked out his imaginary opponent through a potent combination of power and technique. "I'm glad to hear we got some real *fired up* individuals out there ready to go kick 'em out and knock 'em in the teeth! And as your new CEO, I give you permission to do so!"

The crowd went wilder. Jason looked over at Tony, who appeared to be progressing to stage two of his mind control metamorphosis, eyes locked on Kenny G and hanging onto his every word.

Kenny motioned with his hands to calm the crowd.

"Thank you so very much for that *outstanding* introduction! I promise you that as the new CEO for DiNAmite Incorporated, you'll *never* be ashamed to talk about DiNAmite to any of your family or friends or even total strangers *again*! After all, if it's good enough for this ex-Special Forces soldier, then it damn well sure better be good enough for *them*, right!"

"You're right Kenny!" a unison of believers shouted.

"Now after tonight…" Kenny continued, "I expect *all of you* to go out there and convince *everyone* you know – everyone you meet – everyone you see – to drink this stuff! Just look what it's done for me, I'm fighting trim! Look what it's done for so many people in this room here tonight!"

Jason looked around and saw a sea of castaways from the isle of misfits.

"You need to make it your life's mission," Kenny continued with his fighting tirade, "indeed your life's *purpose* to go out there and get this stuff down as many peoples' throats as you possibly can! And remember this while you're doing it: the dinosaurs may be extinct, but that never stopped this Green Beret soldier from living like a T-Rex! Now then, who's ready for a DiNAmite cheer!"

"We're ready Kenny!"

"Alright then, give me a 'D'!"

"D!"

"Give me an 'I'!"

"I!"

"Give me an 'N'!"

"N!"

"Give me an 'A'!"

"A!"

"What's that spell?"

"DiNAmite!"

"I said what's that spell??"

"DiNAmite!"

"I can't heeeaaar you!"

"DiNAmite!"

"Well alright!" Kenny shouted, mission accomplished.

Jason looked over at Tony. "That doesn't spell DiNAmite, that spells Dina."

"Yea, but you know what he means."

6

Stealing the Show

"Dr. Fumonda, there's been a breach in security!" the spectacled nerd in the white lab coat alerted his boss.

"Where? Where's the breach?"

"In Sector 30, sir!"

"Sector 30? Good God!" the boss said, dropping his cup of coffee. "That's where the secret formula is kept! Alert the drones! We need every available backup drone to the front… now!"

"Aye Aye, sir!" the nerd responded and quickly swung into action, grabbing the microphone and alerting everyone in a panic.

"I need every available backup drone to the front! There's been a breach of security in Sector 30! Code Red! Shoot to kill! I repeat, shoot to kill!"

"Sector 30?!" one drone said to another in the hallway. "That sounds like trouble."

"Yea, we better get over there."

"I'm ready to shoot something."

The two drones jogged down the long corridor with their guns and gear: a bag full of grenades disguised as oranges. They saw a strange figure cross in front of them and just as quickly disappear.

"What was that?"

"I don't know, but it was running away from Sector 30."

"Let's go after it."

"You go after it, I'll check on the formula."

"Good plan."

They split up at the end of the hallway. One of the drones turned on his jet pack shoes and rocketed towards the intruder.

Dr. Vaghozi could hear the drone giving him chase and knew he had to turn around quickly and face the drone, or he would never escape alive with the formula.

The drone rocketed around a corner and Vaghozi let him have it, blasting away with a sonic ray gun that sent the drone slamming against a wall.

"Can you hear me now?" Vaghozi said to the drone, who was lying unconscious.

But there was no time to waste and he had to keep running for the exit. Three more drones appeared from his right side. The Doctor flipped a few energetic cartwheels, firing in mid-air as he turned, and quickly dispatched them. He knew there would be more coming if he didn't get out soon.

The alarm was deafening but he kept running, finding a fire exit and diving towards it out into the night. DiNAmite Industries faded in the distance and he made a clean getaway, disappearing from view.

⚓ ⚓ ⚓

"*Hello* ladies..." Tony said from behind his booth at the Americas Food & Beverage Show to two well-dressed young women walking by, a blonde and a brunette who seemed intrigued by DiNAmite's display. "Care to try a little something on the wild side?"

"Um, maybe…" the brunette said to Tony. "We were just on our way over to the Premici exhibit. They're serving alcohol over there. Does yours have alcohol in it?"

"No, but it can if that's what you'd like…" It was an offer less on the wild side and more on the somewhat disturbing *I'll spike your drink with who really knows what* side.

"Well as tempting as that sounds, I think we'll have to pass for now" the blonde said, twinkling her fingers as they waved goodbye.

Jason was taken aback by Tony's unexpected behavior. "What are you gonna do, pull it out of your pocket? We didn't bring anything like that!"

"No I didn't, but Cloe did. It's out in her car." Jason could be such a rule-follower, Tony thought.

"Oh, that would look *really* professional," Jason said. "By the way, where is she?"

"She's in the little girl's room. She'll be right back. I think she's been drinking too much of the product again."

"I think I have been too" Jason said.

"Why, you been hittin' the head a lot?"

"No, it's not that, it's the caffeine I think. I get all jittery at night. Sometimes I find myself getting angry about nothing at all and I'm not even sure why."

"Caffeine does that to some people," Tony said. "Makes them irritable. Don't worry, it's totally normal though."

"I'm not so much worried about my health as I am about some of the thoughts I get when I'm drinking it. I feel much more aggressive, like I have way too much energy.

Except that... well, the other night some guy in the drive-through asks me if I wanted to macho-size my drink and I just felt like I wanted to rip his face off, for no reason at all."

"Really?"

"Yea, it was the weirdest thing. And then I stopped and realized what was going through my mind, and it scared me."

"So did you macho-size it?" Tony asked.

"Yes I did. I didn't want him thinking I wasn't man enough to drink the macho size. Maybe that's what it was: maybe I felt like he was challenging my manhood."

"It's the caffeine bro, don't worry about it. It's just a phase."

"What, like you being gay?"

"Hey, that *was* just a phase" Tony said. "Just a couple of quick experiments and that was it. For a research project."

"That you finished last week."

"In your wet dreams! Or maybe since you can't get Cynthia I really *am* in your wet dreams."

"No, it would take a case of Premici for that to ever happen."

"Just one case, huh?"

"Yep, just one case. Why, does that surprise you?"

"Hey guys!" Cloe shouted as she made her triumphant return from the powder room. "What did I miss?"

"Well, we just signed up a really big client is all..." Tony said.

"You did!" Cloe shrieked. "No way! Who was it?"

Jason was keeping a face as straight as Hugh Hefner,

so Tony decided to keep going with it. "Oh uh, actually it was a couple of young princes from Norway."

"Young princes? Really?"

"Yes" Jason added, "and they want to try some sushi with a nice young American girl."

"Really?!" Cloe squealed in amazement.

"No, not really" Tony replied. "We're just messing with you. Nothing happened while you were gone."

"Oh, *you guys*!" Cloe snorted a laugh and hit Tony on the shoulder. "You had me going there!"

"But you *were* going" Jason said.

"Huh?" Cloe asked, confused.

"Never mind," Jason said. "Look the truth is, it's about to get busy in here as soon as the lunchtime crowd comes in. We need to get our game faces on."

"You got that right Jason" Tony agreed, clapping his hands and rubbing them together. "We need to take advantage of the next couple of hours to sign up a few downlines and get some activity going on here!"

"You got it! Game faces on!" Cloe said, and the three of them prepared to meet the onslaught of convention goers who were sure to pass their way. They had chipped in some money along with Phil and a few others to reserve the booth, and were lucky enough to man it during lunchtime on one of the busiest days of the convention. It was rumored that a huge buyer from Brazil was looking to expand his operations in North America and was going to be in attendance at the show that afternoon, which was sure to increase traffic and make for a high stakes day.

The three of them were prepared with their free samples and marketing materials. They had spent the last week rehearsing their pitch each night over dinner at Applebee's or coffee at Perkins, and were ready to take on the world. The world had begun to trickle in, but would soon flood them with eager participants and curious onlookers.

The clock struck 11:30 and the lunch crowd jammed the floor.

A lady with a 1940s era hairstyle came walking by the booth. Jason quickly snagged her.

"Did you know that the Earth is made up of 75% water?"

"Nah, I didn't know that…" she said, smacking gum loudly in her mouth. "75% huh?"

"It's true" Jason replied. "75% water. And the amazing thing is this: so are our *bodies*."

"For real? Get outta here!"

"I know it sounds hard to believe ma'am, but it's the truth. And you want to know something even *more* amazing? DiNAmite is 75% water also."

Rosie the Riveter was impressed. "So it's all-natural then, huh?" she said, picking up a free sample.

"Oh yes, completely all-natural, ma'am. And good for you, too. We like to say that if it's good for the Earth and good for your body too, you know it just has to be DiNAmite!"

"Hmm…" she said, savoring the flavor in her mouth. Her eyes lit up as she came to a quick conclusion. "Sign me up then!"

"Great!" Jason said. "By the way, what kind of gum is that?"

Cloe was jabbering with a couple of men from Florida in business suits who seemed very interested in these new beverages, remarking that they had not seen them anywhere else before.

"And so these come in different flavors then?"

"Yep! T-Rex Red. Berry Brontosaurus. And my personal favorite: Tri-Me-Orange, as in Triceratops Orange!" she said bubbly.

One of the men cringed. "You might want to have your marketing department work on that last one."

"Which one, the Tri-Me-Orange?"

"Yes. Nobody will know what that means."
"But they'll sure be able to taste it!"

"Right."

"Here, try a sip!" she said, handing a free sample to each of them. Taking the cups in their hand, they swigged it down like whiskey, and smiles of delight came across both their faces.

"This is absolutely wonderful! Where can we buy more?"

"Here, let me get you started!"

Tony was talking to a very serious looking guy who seemed to be writing a book report on the matter.

"Three flavors?" the man asked, eyebrows engaged very seriously.

"That's right, three flavors. And every single one of 'em's got that special key ingredient. It's a patented formula, a little trade secret. But I'll let you in on what it really is…" He leaned forward towards the man, who leaned in to hear Tony.

"It's dinosaur DNA."

The man drew back in great surprise.

"That's why it's called DiNAmite!" Tony said. "It's all natural, 100%, including Dino's DNA. It doesn't get any more natural than that!"

"Yes but death is also natural," replied the man, "and you don't see a rush to sign up for that, now do you?"

Tony only mildly despised the man's inflated sense of cleverness, keeping it well under wraps. "You've got a point there my friend but here, just try some of it" he said, pushing a free sample towards the studious little note-taker. "I think you'll like it."

Taking possession of the free sample, the man at first sniffed it from a guarded distance, and then closer in; finding the courage to sip it gingerly, and finally to conduct a heavy analysis of its flavors, rolling it around in his mouth and coating every part of his tongue for maximum effect.

He smiled brightly, verdict rendered. "That *is* good! How can I sign up for more?"

7

Some 'Splaining

"What do you mean they stole the secret formula! How could they possibly steal the secret formula!" Kenny roared at the top of his lungs.

"We don't know yet how it was done sir," his Lab Chief responded, "but we think it was some kind of a ninja."

"A ninja?"

"Yes sir. Prominent in Japan from the 14th to the 19th centuries, the ninja was capable of extreme feats of unorthodox warfare and a mastery of specialized weapons and tactics. Thought to be extinct after the introduction of gunpowder, the ninja-"

"Look, I don't need a history lesson Schmeckles! I just need to know what happened! Did the ninja kill any of our men? Were there any Chinese throwing stars lodged in anyone's foreheads?"

"No sir, there's no evidence of primitive weapons used. In fact, it's believed that the concussions our folks suffered from were due to some type of a sonic ray gun."

"A sonic ray gun?" Kenny gasped in disbelief. "But that could only mean one thing…"

"The ninjas have upgraded, sir?"

"No, no, no! It means we're dealing with our arch nemesis, the Arizonans!"

"The Arizonans, sir?"

"Yes! It could only be them! It's their weapon of choice, after all! They're a very peaceful lot and wouldn't harm a flea. That's *their* problem, Schmeckles! They're not aggressive enough! They'd rather be destroyed than put up a good fight!"

"You're right, sir. The last one who tried messing with you threw himself over a bridge."

"Threw himself over a bridge?"

"Yea, isn't that what happened?"

"No, he didn't throw himself over, I pushed him over!"

"He was one of those spies, wasn't he?"

"Yes, he was one of those spies. And I think they've probably got one or two more of them around here. Oh trust me, they'll be coming back again to get more of these formulas!" He lowered his voice. "They did only steal one of them, right?"

"Actually sir, they were only able to make off with one of the flavors still in development… Pink Pterodactyl."

Kenny scratched his head in confusion. "Have I approved that flavor? It doesn't sound familiar…"

"No sir, you haven't yet. It hasn't been tested."

"So then what do we do now? We've got a spy out there on the loose with our untested formula."

"We don't know what it will do, sir. Maybe nothing. But if God has his two cents to say about it, I'd say we have a winning formula."

Kenny calmed down to collect his thoughts, temporarily distracted by the inane notion that God would only have a measly two cents.

"So the worst they've done is steal a formula that's

not yet ready for market."

"Yes, that's correct sir."

"So then let's tighten down security here. I want triple security everywhere! And shoot to kill anyone who doesn't remember the password!"

"The password sir?"

"Yes, you remember it, don't you?"

"Yes, of course… of course I do."

"Good! Now then don't let me hear about anymore break-ins around here or I really *will* get upset next time!"

"Understood sir" the Lab Chief gulped. "But sir, about the password thing… maybe we could just stun them? Or give them a little hint first? I mean, killing seems like such a harsh thing to do for just forgetting a little ol' password doesn't it?"

"Nonsense! No one forgets my mother's name at DiNAmite!"

"Ahhh…" the Lab Chief said, relieved. "That is a good point. But won't everyone know where the formula is hidden now? I mean, won't all your downlines find out about it?"

"Are you kidding me? Those stooges have *no idea* about where this stuff's really made or what really goes into it! They think it's *dinosaur* DNA, for Christ's sake! No Schmeckles, they believe what they want to believe. Correction – they believe what I *tell* them to believe! Hell, they think I'm John Wayne with a green beret!"

"You're very admired sir."

"It's more than just admired, Schmeckles! I'm worshipped like a *god*! And truth be told, I might as well be, for all they know!"

Kenny laughed and Schmeckles obligingly laughed

along with him, even though his real name was Fumonda.

╫ ╫ ╫

"Dr. Vaghozi, you *know* you shouldn't have tried to steal the formula all by yourself. It's much too risky!" Povanti badgered her boss, upset by his lone wolf mission.

"Well it's not like any of *you* people were volunteering to help out! You know, it really is true. If you want something done right, you have to do it yourself! I got tired of waiting around, so I decided to take matters into my own hands."

"I would have helped sir," Edison said, "but I was eating dinner."

"All night you were eating dinner, huh?"

"Well, I mean you know me sir… slow eater and all."

"Uh huh. And what about the rest of you? Did you all have dinner plans as well?"

"I didn't," Spigazi responded. "But my phone was shut off last night and I couldn't receive any messages. By the time I got your text I figured it was already too late."

"And why was your phone turned off, Spigazi?"

"Battery was low."

"Well, ain't that just marvelous!" Vaghozi declared. "The most important night *ever* to take place here on Arizona and you had your phone shut off." He pointed to Edison. "And *you* were eating dinner. And who knows what the rest of you were up to."

"Probably no good!" Jones lamely joked and laughed. Vaghozi looked at him with a sour expression on his face, unamused.

Povanti was still upset. "Why did you use the sonic gun, Dr. Vaghozi? You know it's a dead giveaway. Now they'll know who stole the formula for sure."

"I needed the latest equipment for the job. And you all better be on your toes from now on. They'll be looking for us. They'll be looking for that formula too. Edison, Geloriese, Smith: I need a thorough quantum spectrum sequence done on it right away. I want the results on my desk by end of day."

"The pink pterodactyl?"

"That's right, the pink pterodactyl. Dissect that sucker quark by quark. Let's find out exactly what the Krakadons are up to."

"You got it sir."

8 ̶H̶H̶H̶

Prehistoric

It was happy hour at Hooters on a Thursday, and the only thing separating Jason and Tony from the weekend as they munched on cheesy tater tots while taking in the game on TV was that period of time called Friday.

"So Jason," Tony said as he gulped down a swig. "What do you make of Cloe so far? She's doing pretty good with this whole DiNAmite sales thing, huh?"

"Yea, she's actually pretty good. It's surprised me. She's way better than I thought she'd be. And I gotta hand it to you: you saw the potential in her way before I ever did."

"Yea she signed up like 30 new accounts at the trade show."

"You're not kidding either," Jason agreed. "That was like half our total so far."

"More than half. You and me together only signed up less than a dozen!"

"I know, we need to get with it. Still, that's a dozen more than before though."

"I think it's the most successful we've ever been at any venture like this… by far."

"You can say that again," Jason agreed. "And we've tried a bunch of them."

"Yes we have my brother!"

The celebration officially started, Jason chewed pensively on a tater tot. His eyes were watching the movements of the game but his mind was on recent events.

"You know the thing about that trade show…" he said from out of his daze. "It was like… way too easy for us. I mean, sure we had to ante up a hundred bucks each, but look at the return we got from that!"

"Yep, it paid off big time" Tony agreed.

"Yea, it was like all you had to do was get people to try it and they were sold instantly."

"Absolutely. That was the secret."

Jason laughed at the good fortune they had discovered. "I mean, as annoying as I think that Kenny guy is, he was right about one thing: you just have to get it down their throats! The rest of it sells itself."

"Yea, you're right. It was almost like that" Tony said.

The cute waitress stopped by, noticing Jason's glass was nearly empty.

"Can I get you two another one?"

"You sure can" Jason replied. "I'll have another TSS."

"Another Michelob for me please, Bedroom Eyes."

"You got it boys, I'll be back in no time!" she said, winking as she walked away.

"She sure is cute" Jason said.

"She got a real purty mouth" Tony replied.

"She got a real purty everything. I think I'm in love."

"Well, she'll be back," Tony said. "We'll ask her to

sit down with us for a few. Then you can propose to her."

"I don't know," Jason said. "It might be too early for that. I haven't picked out a ring or anything yet."

"She kind of looks like Cynthia a little…"

"You think so?"

"Yes, a little bit. She's got that same hairstyle."

"Yes, that same beautiful hair…" Jason said, his mind seeming to drift off again.

"What's been going on between you two anyway?" Tony asked in between bites. "She ever talk to you at work?"

"No, not really. I think she's avoiding me. Probably afraid I'll ask her out on a tennis date and ruin her game or something."

"I believe that."

"It doesn't matter though," Jason said. "I'm so over her anyway. Right now I'm a little more focused on Bedroom Eyes, to tell you the truth."

"Good choice.   She's sluttier anyway."

"Uh huh, exactly. Hey, even a predatorial stud like me doesn't always have the energy for a complicated hunt."

"Oh you're a predator alright" Tony said, drinking some more.

They finished up their tater tots as the game intensified. It was March Madness and everyone who couldn't get tickets to the big game was glued to their sets to watch the Sun Devils take on the Jayhawks live.

"I have a craving for something sweet" Jason said.

"I know, you told me already. She'll be back in a minute."

"Ha ha. No, I mean something from the menu."

"Oh hey, speaking of sweet. Did you hear about Alice's candy jars?"

"No, what about them?"

"Well you weren't here Monday morning, but when she came into work she had a *horde* of ants just *all over* her candy dishes eating up her M&Ms and her gummy bears and everything else she has in those things."

"No way!"

"Yea, it was pretty nasty. We had to spray all of them too. There was this river of dead ants all along her desk and up the wall going to the outside."

"That's awesome!"

"Yea but good thing she didn't leave any of that candy on our desks, or else we'd have been targeted too."

"She needs to put a lid on those jars or something."

"At least. I'd prefer she just stops with the whole candy shop thing altogether."

"But then no one would ever talk to her."

"Yea, poor thing."

The game went to commercial break. The commercial showed two cavemen from *The Land of the Lost* running from a man-eating dinosaur. One of them pulled out a canned drink from his wooly-haired Fred Flintstone vest, chugged it, and was able to outrun the other. Then the DiNAmite logo appeared on screen.

"No way! Look, it's DiNAmite!" Tony said.

"Yes I see that, during March Madness even! That's gotta be expensive."

'… Berry Brontosaurus and Tri-Me-Orange. So drink the only energy drink with *real* dinosaur DNA that's guaranteed to give you fast energy *whenever* you need it. DiNAmite. Put a Little Prehistoric in Your Step.'

"Wow dude, that was awesome!" Tony said.

"Yea it was! It was a pretty short commercial but I mean… at least we're advertising now."

"Right," Tony said, "now that Kenny's in charge we're seeing a lot of changes for the better. Speaking of changes for the better, don't look now but here comes Bedtime Eyes."

9 ⌗

Growths

Cynthia and her Russian friend Bossanova were playing tennis at Encanto Park, bright and early on another beautiful Saturday morning. It was perfect tennis weather: sunny and not too hot, with a faint cool breeze. Bossanova smacked a forehand to Cynthia's backhand side. Cynthia returned fire with a winner cross-court.

"Aghh!" Bossanova groaned. "I should know better than test you that side! Is not good for me!" she said in Russianglish.

"But it's good for me!" Cynthia laughed. "Keep testing me, B!"

They both laughed and played another rally, warm-up for the upcoming USTA tournament they were both taking part in. Having met a few years ago, they had since become regular hitting partners, religiously playing every Saturday morning when the weather was good. Cynthia had played in college but this was her first USTA event, while Bossanova was a regular on the USTA circuit and competed in as many tournaments as she possibly could.

"Arrrgggh!" Bossanova grunted as she smacked another forehand with incredible power, hitting it with such force that Cynthia had no time to react.

"Wow, B! Where did *that* come from?" Cynthia gasped in amazement. The ball traveled so fast past Cynthia that she could hear it sizzle like a bullet.

"Oh, just so much energy, you know!" Bossanova laughed. "Proper diet exercise nutrition supplement." She had the annoying habit of mangling all her keywords together into one soupy sentence, without the benefit of any coherent grammatical structure.

"Well, it seems like it's working for you."

The burly Russian grabbed a ball from her pocket and hit it to Cynthia to begin another rally. "Yes, is energy drink which provides super strength called 'DiNAmite'."

"Excuse me, did you say 'DiNAmite'?" Cynthia asked, distracted and allowing the ball to fly past her.

"Yes, DiNAmite. Why, you know this drink?"

"Well… yea I do" she replied in amazement. "You know the guy at work that I was telling you about who's always hitting on me… you know, the one we saw here that time? He uses it."

"Jason?"

"Yes, Jason. You remember. He and his other friend were trying to get me to go to one of their little events where they wanted to sell me some of it."

"And you said no?"

"Of course I said no! I wouldn't go with those two! Did you see how *bad* they were?"

"Yes I did. So you should go with me then" Bossanova said as they walked to the bench to take a water break.

"Why, are you really into it too?" Cynthia asked.

"Oh yes. Drink gallons daily. So, *sooo* good for you!"

"It is, huh?"

"Oh yes! Not drinking anything else anymore, just this" she said, taking a can of DiNAmite out of her backpack, Tri-Me Orange.

"Orange flavor?" Cynthia asked. "Is it good?"

"Oh my God yes! Tastes so, so good! Refreshing drink vitalizes giving good strength!" the Russian enthused. She was sweating profusely and had to wipe her face off with a towel. Then she removed her headband to replace it with a dry one, which exposed a very noticeable projection sticking out from her forehead.

"Oh my God, B! Is that a horn growing out of your head?" Cynthia gasped in shock.

Bossanova felt around until she located the pointy object.

"Yes this thing, not sure what is. Started growing couple days ago. Yes, think is horn growing sharper."

Cynthia was aghast. "Well… don't you think you should maybe get that checked out by somebody?" she said, horrified.

"Oh no, no, no! Is good! Never feel better in all my live long day! This drink cure *everything*! Here, try some!"

╫ ╫ ╫

Jason and Tony received an urgent phone call from Phil, and it was apparent that they needed to meet him at Hooters right away. In most cases this would have made for a really poor reason to leave work early, but this time something was different. Phil was not himself.

"So what'd he sound like?" Jason asked as they got into the Jeep. It was ten minutes before 5:00. "Did he sound scared? Confused?"

"I don't know, I mean he just seemed to be in a state

of panic, really" Tony replied as he backed out of the parking space and put it in gear. "Said he needed to talk to us about something really important."

"Wonder how long he's been there?" Jason asked.

"Probably since lunch."

"Yea, knowing him he's been there a while already. Probably way drunk by now. ·Either that or the crisis on his hands is that he can't decide between which Hooters chick to sleep with next."

"Yes that would be a crisis. I wish I had that kind of crisis" Tony said.

"Come on, Phil's just got the swagger thing going on. Way more swagger than either of us has. That's how he gets all the chicks. Or should I say floozies."

"Floozies?" Tony said as he turned a corner and sped up. "That's not what you were calling Miss Bedtime Eyes the other day."

"I was drunk" Jason replied. "And besides, I only wanted to take her out sometime just as friends. Nothing more."

"Oh of course, as friends!" Tony laughed.

"Yes, friends. She could use a little direction in her life. A little good advice."

"Oh, so now you want to come in and rescue her. Sort of the fatherly figure type, huh. I didn't know you had that much Savior in you" Tony said.

"Maybe just a little."

They approached Hooters and found a great parking spot next to the front entrance.

"Must be my lucky day" Tony said as he pulled in.

"Let's hope our luck continues inside."

"Oh come on, you know luck inside *that* place is directly proportional to the size of your bank account."

"Or maybe the size of something else" Jason said confidently.

"You wish."

"Yea, I do" Jason admitted.

They walked to the front door and Jason grabbed the handle to pull it open. "I just hope he's not too drunk to talk."

"Me too" Tony agreed.

They went inside and found Phil at a booth, hunched over the menu as if he had passed out, a half-gone beer next to his sagging head.

"Phil!" Jason said, touching him on the shoulders. "Everything okay buddy?"

His head rolled to the left and then skyward. There was life. "Oh, hey guys! Thanks for coming on such short notice."

"No problem" Jason answered. "We thought you were asleep or something."

"Huh? Oh yea, right. Right" Phil said, seeming confused. "Yea, I was just taking a quick nap. Just thinking about some things too."

"Why, what's on your mind?" Jason asked as he and Tony took a seat in the booth across from him.

"Yea, anything we can help you with?" Tony asked, removing his coat and looking for the waitress to order a drink. "Everything okay with the business?"

"Huh? Oh yea, yea. Yea everything's fine" Phil replied, still coming out of his daze. "Everything's fine except... well, maybe *I'm* not so fine."

"What do you mean?" Jason asked. "Have you had

too much to drink again?"

"Phil, we need to think about getting you some kind of help if this keeps up" Tony said, the threat of intervention lurking just beneath the concern in his voice. "I mean, you're here almost every day."

"Yea Phil" Jason agreed. "We're your friends. You can count on us to help you. Oh Tony, here comes the waitress."

She was carrying a plate full of buffalo hot wings and set it down next to Phil. "Here you are sweetie. Can I get you two boys started with something?" Party Girl was her name.

"Oh, I'm sure you easily could, Party Girl" Tony said. "I'll have the usual."

"Me too" Jason said.

"Great, two usuals coming right up then!" she laughed. "Any appetizers to start with? More wings maybe?"

Phil's eyes were closed as if he had passed out again but he began sniffing the air very loudly, seeming to be aware of the buffalo wings in front of his face by its powerful meaty aroma. Party Girl stopped to look at him as his sniffing grew louder. His tongue flickered in and out of his mouth. Jason was growing embarrassed.

"Phil, if you want to eat it it's – "

Phil lunged for the plate with his face and snapped at the buffalo wings, retrieving two of them dangling from his lips. Throwing his head back like a bird to allow the chicken meat to fall more securely into his smacking mouth, he began chewing ferociously, as if he hadn't eaten for days, making loud gulping and grunting noises. Party Girl was horrified.

"Oh my God!" she said. "What's wrong with him?

He's not getting anymore to drink! That was just way too creepy…" and she hurried off.

"Agreed!" Jason said, angry with Phil for his outlandish behavior. "Phil, what the Hell was that all about!"

"Yea, how much have you been drinking?" Tony asked.

Raw chicken bones fell out of Phil's mouth as he licked his lips. He had pulled all the usable meat off the bones without even once using his hands. Buffalo sauce was all over his face and he was a drunken mess.

"I'm sorry, I just don't know what's gotten into me, boys" he said with a burp.

"Phil, here wipe your face off!" Jason said, handing him a few napkins.

"I mean…" Phil said, "I don't know what's been happening. That's why I called you guys down here. I'm scared."

Tony looked over at Jason and they were both perplexed.

"You're scared Phil?" Tony asked. "Of what? What's there to be scared about?"

"Of all the weird things that have been going on" Phil answered, trying to recollect his composure, which was thoroughly scattered by now. "Strange things have been happening to me. I get these urges that I can't explain. Like that whole thing I just did with these wings. I can't explain any of that! It's like I'm just an observer and I have no control over any of it!"

Tony looked over at Jason to see if he was making any sense of it. For Jason, it was all too familiar, minus the disgusting displays of misbehavior. He had experienced some of those very same unexplained urges to do things that were completely out of character. The macho size drink incident was just one of them. And then a connection hit him.

"I wonder if it's related to the DiNAmite?" he asked. "I mean, I told you about this the other day, Tony, about how I've been having all these violent urges that I have to try to keep under control somehow? We thought it might be related to all the caffeine in the DiNAmite!"

"That's right, I do remember you telling me about that!" Tony said.

"How much of it have you been drinking, Phil?" Jason asked. "I mean, maybe it's been causing the same kind of problems with you?"

Phil just laughed, as if resigned to his fate. "Oh, it's gallons and gallons of it every day, boys! I'm addicted to it! I can't get enough of it! It gets me in touch with my prehistoric side, you know that!" He was speaking sloppily and burping intermittently. "I honestly couldn't live without it! Plus, just think of all the points I'm racking up by drinking that much! I'll be Diamond level in no time! Kenny will personally invite me over to take a ride in one of those cars of his! You boys just watch and learn!" he yelled, capping off his role model speech with a loud belch.

Jason began having second thoughts about the whole DiNAmite thing, if it meant ending up like Phil, and began to wonder if he himself was addicted. A thought occurred to him that until now had only seemed a curious oddity: no one in the organization even knew where the drink was made. How could anyone really know what its ingredients were? Was it dinosaur DNA, or just an excess of caffeine that had turned Phil into such a drooling, snapping disaster?

"By the way," Jason asked, "where's it made anyway? I've always wondered that. Maybe Kenny would tell you Phil, if you ever get to drive his car."

"I think it's made right here locally" Tony said.

"That's the beauty of it!" Phil replied drunkenly and very loudly, apparently re-energized after his quick snack of wings. "Nobody knows where *any* of it's made! Oh sure, they have a factory here, but it's not where the key ingredient comes from: the dinosaur DNA. It gets shipped in from god knows where! But we don't need to know, boys! We just need to keep drinking more and more of it, and to get others to drink more and more of it! That's the whole point! That's why we're all here!"

"I have to go" Jason said. "Come on Tony, let's get out of here."

"You sure?" Tony asked, unsure of whether they should just leave him there.

"Here" Jason said, handing Phil a ten dollar bill. "Give this to Party Girl for us. I just remembered I have to be somewhere."

"Okay!" Phil said, laughing. "You boys have a DiNAmite evening then!" He was slurring his speech and barely able to get the words out.

As they got up to leave Tony tripped on something protruding out from underneath the table. It was greenish in color and looked scaly, like snake skin. Tony got closer to take a look and could see that it appeared to be connected to Phil's rear end somehow.

"Phil… what the fuck is *that*?" Tony asked.

Phil just chuckled some more and looked down beneath the table.

"Oh *that*? That's my new tail! Had it for a few days now! How do you boys like my tail!"

10 ╫╫╫

Monty Meets His Match

The two health inspectors wore dark suits and dark sunglasses and looked like they meant serious business. Sent out by the government on reports of suspicious activity at the facility, a quick check of the records indicated that the DiNAmite plant had somehow eluded all previous FDA inspections. There was no written documentation of any kind. But Monty and Jake were determined to change all that.

They were two of the hardest-nosed and by-the-book agents that the federal government had ever booked on its payroll. If there were violations to be found of any kind whatsoever within the facility, Uncle Sam could trust that Monty and Jake would find them. There wasn't a sub-temperature soup or an allergen-contaminated glove that could escape their vigilant eye. The other agents on the health inspection force called them Money and Bank, because it was as good as gold that wherever they went, the place would be closed until serious violations were corrected. Sometimes they were never corrected.

Stepping outside of the government-issued sedan and eyeing the outside of the building, they spotted a dozen different ways to shut 'em down. Trash uncollected near the front entrance: sanitary violation. Part of the roof in need of repair: environmental contamination. The painted lines on the parking spaces near the loading dock not clearly defined:

logistics and receiving hazard.

"Let's go inside, see what kind of numbers we can run up" Monty said confidently. Jake nodded in agreement. They took their work very seriously, always challenging themselves to find more violations in the current inspection than in the previous one; exemplifying the mark of a true professional to never be satisfied with what's been done in the past and to never rest on one's laurels.

"May I help you?" the secretary behind the desk at the front door asked the two of them as they entered the facility.

"You certainly can, ma'am" Monty said, taking off his sunglasses. "Name's Inspector Monty. This is my partner, Inspector Jake. We're here today to pay a visit to the facility and provide a complimentary health inspection."

The secretary was only mildly surprised. She'd seen them here before, the government types, and she recognized by their dark suits and the dark sedan they drove that they were here to do some sort of inspection. She just couldn't figure out why they kept sending them here every so often. Did they really need that many health inspections for one facility?

"Oh my! A complimentary inspection, you say?"

"That's right ma'am. Free of charge" Monty replied.

"Oh, well then… I better ring Kenny."

"Kenny?" Monty asked.

"Yes. He's our new CEO. Uh, please hold for a second while I put you through" she said, speaking to them as if she were on the phone with them. Kenny picked up.

"Uh, Kenny?" she said into the phone, "Yes, it's Jan up front. There are two members here from the health inspection agency and they wish to have a look around, free of charge." She covered the phone and asked them "did I say that right?"

"Yes, that about sums it up" Monty replied.

"Oh, right *now* you say?" she said. "Oh, okay, I'll send them in right away then."

She hung up the phone. "You can go right on in there gentlemen, right through those doors" She pointed to two large, gate-style wooden doors. "Kenny will be with you shortly."

"Great, thank you Jan" Monty said and smiled, as both he and Jake walked over to the doors, opened them, and went inside.

It was dark inside and looked something like out of a horror film, with a fusty foyer that made for a very poor transition to a clean factory, if it was to be a clean factory at all.

"Look at this place," the normally reserved Jake said. "Just crawling with countless violations."

"Yes, thousands of them" Monty replied as he saw a spider cross a web in a corner of the room.

A side door opened and Kenny came bounding out, full of energy as always.

"Howdy, gentlemen! What can I do ya for?" he said very excitedly, obviously hopped up on something.

"Oh hello… you must be Kenny?" Monty said.

"That I am, my friend! Kenny Graham, Special Forces Retired and now CEO of DiNAmite!"

"Yes, nice to meet you Kenny. I'm Inspector Monty, and this is my partner, Inspector Jake."

"Howdy" Kenny acknowledged Jake.

"Listen," Monty pressed. "We don't have a lot of time to waste, so let's get started, shall we? We're here to inspect for health code violations."

"Violations, eh?" Kenny said, eyeing them suspiciously, belligerence carefully guarded. "You mean like… violations as in when someone broke in the other night and stole one of our formulas, that sort of a violation? You two wouldn't know anything about that, now would you?"

"No, no, no, we're not here to check out your security set-up. Just health code" Monty replied.

"Uh huh… sure you are" Kenny said, seeming to agree on the surface but subtly making them aware that he was on to them. He knew they had to be associated with the break-in somehow. Perhaps they didn't get what they needed the first time, and the two of them were sent back to scout out other potential vulnerabilities in the network and where they might find other secrets. "Come right this way," Kenny said, "I want to take you over to Sector 30."

"Sector 30?" Jake asked, baffled by the awkward naming convention for a manufacturing facility.

"Uh huh. Why, are you familiar with it?" Kenny asked, winking at him. "That's where we keep all the good stuff, as you guys might remember. You won't want to miss any of that. Here, come this way."

Kenny led them outside the foyer and into a very long hallway. They began walking down it, a narrow passage marked by an endless series of doors on either side.

"This place used to be an insane asylum, if you can believe that. Bet the two of you didn't know that."

"No, we had no idea" Monty responded. "In fact, there's no record of any inspection ever being done on this place."

"Oh, there have been inspections. Lots of them" Kenny said. "You guys probably just lost the paperwork."

"I don't think so" Monty replied firmly.

"Well I can only imagine…" Kenny said slyly, "that those crazy folks were probably seeing lots of *pink pterodactyls* when they did their inspections… if you know what I mean…"

The two agents were bewildered. "No, not really" Jake said, confused. "Anyway, can we just get on with the inspection please?"

"Oh yes, yes of course" Kenny replied. Here, just right behind this door." He opened a plain steel door for them. "I want to show you something." He followed them in and closed the door shut behind him.

Then he said sternly, "There is no record, my Arizonan friends… because there is no one who ever lives to tell about it."

"What?"

Jan up at the front desk could hear faint screams of horror. She took the pencil out of her mouth she'd been chewing on and just shook her head. "Hmm, must have found roaches again."

11 ⌗

Your Codename is Starbuck

Tony was in a hurry to share the news the next morning at Murman. He approached Cloe's desk and spoke to her in an excited whisper.

"Cloe, you're not gonna believe what Jason and I had to go through last night!"

It was still early in the morning and hardly anyone had shown up yet, but Tony believed that with something this crazy, it was important no one else besides Cloe hear him. He knew that she, at least, would not jump to the conclusion that he had become completely unhinged.

"What, what happened?" Cloe asked. Simply based on Tony's strange behavior it was apparent that something very unusual had taken place.

"Well, so Jason and I met with Phil – you remember Phil, right?"

"Yes, your upline, of course."

"I mean, I know you haven't seen much of him. But anyway so Jason and I meet up with him over at Hooters last night. We go in and he's just sitting there just smashed, all slumped over his beer and drooling."

"Oh my God!"

"Yea, so that's not the worst part of it. He starts talking about how all this weird shit's happening to him and he doesn't know what's going on and all this and that and *then* – then the waitress comes over."

Jason was just getting in and saw the two of them talking. He walked over to join the conversation.

"Are you guys talking about Phil?"

"Yea, I was just explaining what happened last night."

"Weird shit" Jason said, to prepare Cloe.

"Oh my God!" Cloe said, getting very excited.

"Yea so the waitress comes over," Tony continued, "and sets down this plate full of hot wings."

"Phil's almost passed out by this time" Jason said.

"Right, he's almost passed out, but he starts making these loud snorting noises, like he's a fucking werewolf or something."

Cloe's eyes widened at the bizarre story.

"And *then* he snaps at the plate in front of him like a lizard and grabs up a couple pieces of chicken in his mouth and just starts chowing down on 'em – no hands, nothing – just his bare teeth! Makes this huge mess *all* over his face with the sauce flying *everywhere*." Tony paused for dramatic effect. "And then he says to us 'oh yea, I don't know what just happened' just like that, like nothing unusual happened or anything!"

"Well," Jason said, "but I mean he *knows* something weird's going on. He just doesn't know what it is yet."

"Yea, who does" Tony agreed. "But here's the part that made me want to run for the door. We were already on our way out, but this sealed the deal for both of us, right Jason?"

"Oh yes it did" Jason concurred. "You gotta hear this Cloe."

"Oh my God!" Cloe said.

"So I get up to leave," Tony continued, "and I nearly trip over something. Well, come to find out the guy's got a… fucking stegosaurus tail, growing out of his ass or something. I don't really know what it was but it was green and scaly and really freaky."

"And he said to us, 'how do you like my new tail, guys? I've had it a few days now' as we were leaving," Jason said, "kind of like an 'oh by the way' thing, like nothing really unusual about that. And I'm thinking, 'Phil, isn't that something you should have mentioned to us, kind of more upfront?'" Jason said. "He just kept laughing, and so we left. I haven't talked to him since then."

"Me neither" Tony said.

"Oh my God! Are you guys serious?" Cloe asked. "You guys aren't putting me on again, are you?"

"No way, serious as cancer" Tony said. "It happened."

"Yes, it did happen" Jason agreed. "Sure as we're standing here. Phil's turning into a… well, I don't know what he's turning into but he needs to get it checked out by somebody."

"And you don't think he was putting you guys on, do you?" Cloe asked.

"No, that tail seemed pretty real to me" Tony replied.

"Yea, and plus he couldn't fake the whole thing with the buffalo wings, that was just crazy. Oh – here comes Swagley, better get to work" Jason said, and casually left the area to go back over to his desk.

"See you later Cloe" Tony said, following closely behind Jason.

"Okay, bye!"

They headed back over to their cubicles, mentioning purchase order numbers. Swagley didn't like to see groups of employees gabbing, and he was always grumpy in the morning until his third cup of coffee.

As Jason approached his desk the phone began ringing. He hated it when assholes called him this early in the morning, before he even had time to grab a cup of coffee himself.

"Hi, this is Jason" he picked up.

A voice that sounded vaguely familiar said "Listen to me carefully. I know where the DiNAmite is made. Follow my instructions closely. The fate of the world hangs in the balance."

⚞⚞⚞

After work, Jason followed the instructions to the tee, as he was instructed to do. The mystery caller had warned him not to tell anyone else about the meeting before it took place, not even his best friend Tony. He was to meet a man named Vaghozi at a local coffee shop to discuss a matter of grave importance. The gravity of the situation began to weigh on him; the man on the phone had said that the fate of the entire world was hanging in the balance. He didn't explain why Jason was chosen to play a critical role, but in situations like these Jason knew he just had to run with it. You can't ask too many questions when you're saving the world, you just do it.

It wasn't as though the turn of events was a complete surprise. Jason had seen the troubling signs and knew that something terrible was going on. In his own experiences he was having these strange urges to become violent for no apparent reason. Tony had attributed it to the excess of caffeine in the DiNAmite, but Jason wasn't so sure anymore.

After meeting with Phil in the restaurant last night, it was obvious that strange events were taking place. DiNAmite had just begun to kick off its national television advertising campaign into high gear, just as Kenny Graham took over as CEO. It was well known by those familiar with DiNAmite that it would put a little prehistoric in your step, he just never suspected until last night that it might also turn you into a groundhog. Punxsutawney Phil. Now that he thought about it, perhaps it was all starting to make sense.

He parked at the Starbucks where Vaghozi was to meet him and cautiously went inside, eyeing every customer in the place for his man. If things went south and he were somehow the unsuspecting victim of an evil plot to take over the world, then at least he would have witnesses to his demise. They can't kill all of us in here, Jason figured as he ordered up a Venti Java Chip Frappuccino. Or maybe they could. But he was comforted by the fact that at least he would go out in style, his bullet-riddled body perhaps slumped tastefully over an interesting chess game, next to the display promoting sustainable agriculture in Burkina Faso.

The barista was slim and attractive, with an almost unrealistic, cartoon-like physique. Her nametag said *Povanti*, an unusual name for such an usual looking barista. She whipped Jason's frap into a foamy froth, handing the finished drink over to him with a flirtatious wink and a smile.

"I spiked it with a little something extra."

"You did?" Jason laughed, forgetting for a moment about the fate of the world hanging in the balance.

"Uh huh, go on, try it."

"Okay" he smiled, and sipped some of the drink. It tasted like every other Java Chip Frappuccino he'd ever had.

"Whatever you put in it, it's working" he said, playing along with her joke.

"I'm glad to hear it. Well, I have to help the next customer now. It was nice meeting you" she smiled coyly.

"Likewise."

"Uh… Jason?" a voice called out from behind him. It was friendly-sounding enough.

He turned around to see who was calling his name, knowing that it had to be his secret contact. He imagined the man would be wearing spy sort of gear: a hat, sunglasses, and trench coat. But it was nothing of the sort. He was a much older man than he had anticipated, and had that mad scientist appearance of someone who wouldn't at all be out of place in a Hollywood movie set. He looked around for the cameras as he began to wonder if Tony had set him up to be punk'd.

"Yes, I'm Jason. Dr. Vaghozi, I presume?"

"Yes, you presume correctly. I am Dr. Vaghozi" the man said, shaking Jason's hand warmly. "I'm sure you're wondering why I've asked you to come here and meet with me."

"Well, yes I am. I mean you said on the phone that it was very important, and that the fate of the world was hanging in the balance."

"It is" Vaghozi confirmed gravely. "You see, I represent an elite team of soldier-scientists who have been sent here from another planet to save the Earth from being taken over by a vicious alien species bent on the destruction of all freedom-loving civilizations in this galaxy."

Jason almost choked on his frappuccino. "You what?"

"I know it sounds strange but listen to me, Jason. My team needs access to the circle of influence that you have through your connections with the DiNAmite organization in order to reverse the situation and set back the plans of the Converters."

"The Converters?" Jason asked, grimacing as a mild brain freeze from the frappuccino began locking up his head. He had always heard that if you tilt your head sideways it was supposed to help. It was in this way that he listened to what Vaghozi had to say next.

"Yes, the Converters. The Converters are the vanguard of the reptilian-like alien species that's been sent to this planet in order to begin the process of preparing for the mass invasion that's sure to come within the next couple of months, and it's of the utmost importance that we stop them here on this planet before they can do anymore damage. If they take the Earth, they'll have a strategic foothold on this entire section of the galaxy and a launching pad for future attacks against other nearby planetary civilizations."

Jason was buzzing from his flavored coffee drink, which had the effect of intensifying the mystery of the story.

"Are you for real?" he asked.

"Yes, I'm completely for real. Here, let me prove it to you. Are you prepared to see something that no human being has ever before seen in the history of mankind?"

"Does it involve taking off your pants?"

"My pants? No, nothing of the sort. I'm talking about giving you an insight into what's going on behind the scenes of this inter-galactic struggle, up close and personal."

Jason had come this far, all the way to Starbucks. He wasn't about to stop now. Not with the fate of mankind resting on his shoulders. "Okay, why not. Let's me see what you're talking about."

"Excellent. Then let's step outside and we'll be there in no time."

The two of them left the café and went out into the parking lot.

"Here's my ride" Vaghozi said, pointing to a green 1992 Dodge Stealth. "Get in and we'll be there in no time."

Jason got in the car and Vaghozi fired up the engine.

"Do they still make these things?" Jason asked.

"Not any like *these*" Vaghozi said smiling mischievously, putting the car in gear and easing out of the parking lot.

"Why, does this one have more power than the others? Dual-Overhead Cam, right?" Jason asked.

"And then some" Vaghozi replied, opening up the throttle and accelerating to 50 miles per hour in seconds. "She's definitely got a lot more power than the usual make of this vehicle. I'll show you what I mean in just a minute."

"Okay, but just don't get too crazy. I want to live after all, if I'm going to help save the planet" he said, finishing up the last of his coffee drink.

They drove for a couple of minutes before Vaghozi found an open road without a car in sight.

"Here comes the power part. Hang on to your seat." He switched gears into Overdrive and the car lurched into the air, taking off like an airplane. Jason's jaw dropped as the car transformed itself into a flying orb before his very eyes. The console dash became a lighted instrumentation panel.

"This is a UFO car! Holy shit!" Jason cried out. "I can't believe I'm riding in a UFO with an alien!"

Vaghozi smiled and punched in a few lighted buttons on the instrumentation panel. "I'm setting a course for Headquarters. We'll be there in five seconds from now, your time."

Jason could see green lights that seemed to emanate from the underside of the craft and glow on the cloud tops. They were already at an extremely high altitude. To Jason, time seemed to come to a near standstill and he seemed to be moving in slow motion. His brain was fully aware of the altered passage of time, but it was as if his body was a separate entity from his thoughts and his mind. He could see the traveling ship from the outside looking in, as if watching it on film.

Before he had much time to think about it, they were already landing. All Jason could see was the craft approaching the ground among a landscape of ice sheets and glaciers.

"Where are we?" Jason asked.

"Somewhere in your continent known as Antarctica. This is where Headquarters is."

"Get out! Do you always have to go this far? I mean from Arizona out to here?"

"Oh, not all the time. We have a Forward Operating Base we call the 'Shack' located in Wickenburg, not far from DiNAmite. But this is where most of my team and our equipment are located."

"But why Antarctica? It's so cold here."

"Not really, we have ways of staying warm. Besides, the Krakadons would never suspect us here. They'd think we'd probably set up on the moon if we ever came to Earth to stop them."

"The Krakadons? Who are they?"

"They're the nasty reptilian-like alien species who are trying to destroy us all: your Converter friends from DiNAmite are just the vanguard of their operation. They've completely taken over Krakadoa, your planet Mars. The DiNAmite plant in Phoenix is their first facility on Arizona -

uh, that's our name for your planet. That's where they spew their filth from, but we've recently learned that they have big plans for expansion. Come on, let's go out and meet the team."

"Okay. But why do you call Earth 'Arizona'?"

Vaghozi sighed, as if there was too much to say. "It's a long story, Starbuck, full of wonderful hopes and miserable wars. Perhaps it's best to tell you another time."

They stepped out of the green orb craft and onto the tarmac. It was a huge underground facility, somewhere beneath the giant frozen continent, where apparently it was difficult to detect alien operations. Vaghozi's team of elite soldier-scientists was waiting to greet them on the runway.

"Hello, Jason! I'm Povanti, you might remember me…" a slender looking female said, looking straight out of Aeon Flux, complete with the whole black, skin-tight get-up. Jason realized it was the same barista who had served him the spiked drink at Starbucks. "I'm the chief intelligence officer."

"Hello…" Jason said, confused. "But… weren't you just at Starbucks, serving me the drink?"

"Indeed I was, at the time. Did you enjoy it?"

"Oh, yes of course. I think. I mean, I didn't get to drink that much of it, really."

"Yes, the TSS is potent," Vaghozi pressed, "and it's quite literally kept ice cold here, in a perfectly preserved cryogenic state. But anyway Jason, perhaps you better meet some of the others, for we haven't a lot of time. Please folks, make friends with Jason Newcastle."

The others took turns introducing themselves.

"I'm Spigazi, chief weapons officer."

"Geloriese, chief scientist."

"Smith, medical officer."

"Edison, navigational officer."

"Jones, communications specialist."

"And I, of course, am Dr. Vaghozi, formerly a Colonel in our civilization's defense force. They dusted me off and took me out of retirement just for this mission. I have a history here on Arizona, and so they felt I would be the right one for the job."

"Jason it's absolutely critical that you help us" Povanti said. "Our time is running short and we don't have long before the Krakadons take over this world."

"Yes, they've already started their terraforming operations," Geloriese said, "so it won't be long before they are unstoppable."

"Terraforming? Is that like, growing grass and stuff?"

"Yes, that's a part of it," Geloriese said, "only the Krakadons prefer swampy, humid wetlands."

"That should be quite a challenge on a planet as big as Earth" Jason scoffed.

"Oh, it's not as difficult as you might think" Vaghozi interjected. "It can be done in a relatively short amount of time, with the right equipment. This entire headquarters here? Created in about two weeks using fully autonomous constructabots working nonstop day and night. Complete with facilities for food, water, and shelter."

"Wow…" Jason said, looking out again at the vast indoor airbase. The idea that robotic Caterpillars had created the thing in only two weeks was mind boggling. "But what is it you need me to do exactly? How am I supposed to help save the planet?"

"Well, we need to keep things on the down-low for

right now" Vaghozi replied, and Jason wondered how a Dodge Stealth floating in the air in a heavily populated area could be anything other than on the up-high. Vaghozi continued. "The only two persons that you can tell about this for now are your friends Tony and Cloe. They both have some experience with DiNAmite, and neither one of them has been converted yet."

"Converted? You mean by the Converters" Jason asked.

"Yes, Jason. But what I really mean – and haven't told you so far – is that they haven't yet been converted into a Krakadon."

"You see," Povanti began to explain, "the whole thing about DiNAmite is not that it contains any dinosaur DNA. It doesn't. But it *does* contain Krakadon DNA. So what they're essentially doing is slowly turning humans into Krakadons over the course of time, by having them drink this DiNAmite liquid, which is acting as a sort of catalyst for DNA change, systematically transcribing and replacing bits and pieces of human DNA with their own DNA. Typically the change is slow enough not to be noticeable, but lately they've been increasing the dosage in an attempt to hurry up and complete the transcription process for the entire human race. Our intelligence indicates that they may think they're running out of time. They probably know that we're onto them."

"Which would make sense," Vaghozi said, "because we're about three times as intelligent as they are."

"But you guys look just like us" Jason said. "I mean, I can't tell you apart from anyone."

"Nor can you tell the Krakadons from anyone" Vaghozi replied. "We both have to take a special serum to appear to be human. Once we stop taking the serum, however, we turn back into our original selves within days."

"You're kidding me, right? So, are you guys hideously ugly or what?" Jason asked.

"No, we're actually quite good looking" Povanti replied.

"We are" Vaghozi agreed. "Some might say better looking even. We're super-intelligent... and we've managed to engineer certain of our body parts to be, let's say... bigger, or more perkier."

"The ladies say my engineered parts are the biggest" Jones said.

"Alright Jones, let's not start with that" Vaghozi said. "We're at war with the Krakadons, and we need your help, Jason."

"I'm ready to help."

"Excellent" Vaghozi replied. "We're working on the antidote formula right now as we speak, and we hope to have it completed within days. Once we have the antidote formula ready to go, we'll crystallize it into chip form... and we'll need *you* to sneak it into the DiNAmite facility and throw it into their mixing pool. They've tightened up security there and we can't do it by brute force alone."

"You need *me* to do that? But I'm not exactly qualified for that type of work."

"We'll be there as your backup, in case things go badly" Povanti said. "But it's you who has the influence at DiNAmite to make it happen."

"I do?" Jason asked.

"Yes," Povanti continued, "through your connection with Phil, your so-called 'upline'. He's already been converted, so there's nothing we can do for him now until we get the antidote, but we need you to talk him into giving you a tour inside the facility, so that you can install the crystal chip, when the time is right. What's so funny?" she asked, noticing Jason's smirk.

"Oh, you just reminded me of a Doors song, that's all" Jason said, straightening himself up. "But it's nothing, sorry. Anyway listen, Phil's waaay gone. It's kind of dangerous to even be around him."

"We know, but we'll have your back in case anything goes down" Vaghozi said. "But – just remember to keep this on the down-low. And you can't allow Phil and the Krakadons to suspect that there's anything unusual going on, or they might start to investigate *you*. Keep buying their products. Don't let your PV slip."

"My PV?"

"Your personal volume. It's one of those Multi-Level Marketing terms that means the amount of crap you're buying for your own personal consumption."

"I'll try not to let it slip."

"Great, then let's get you back to the Shack. But first we'll need to get you decontaminated before you go back, so that nothing is compromised. Come on, let's get moving, Starbuck."

"What's this 'Starbuck' thing you're calling me?"

"Oh," Vaghozi said to Jason, "we've decided that that's our new codename for you."

"It's kind of cute" Povanti said.

"Really cute" Jones added.

"Don't get any ideas, Jones" Spigazi said.

"But I just got here!" Jason said, disappointed. "Damn, I always knew if I ever visited Antarctica I wouldn't be staying long."

"You'll need to get completely undressed and use our decon shower. Povanti can assist you with that."

"But did I mention I'm really glad you chose me?"

╫ ╫ ╫

Back in Phoenix, Vaghozi was only able to give a quick tour of the Shack before pressing issues forced an early cancellation. The veteran soldier-scientist hurriedly took Jason back to the Starbucks parking lot.

"Gotta go! We'll be in touch!" Vaghozi said, speeding away in his green Dodge Stealth, the perfect vehicle for a road trip to mid-life crisis or a barren ice sheet. Where he was going or why he had to leave so soon was still a mystery to Jason. Perhaps he had been hypnotized and the old man had probed him for scientific understanding and was now completely done with him.

He waved goodbye and looked at his watch. Only an hour had passed since he first arrived at Starbucks, before he even knew the name Vaghozi. And yet in that short amount of time he'd had an entire venti frappuccino - and been to Antarctica and back.

"I gotta tell Tony about this" he said, getting into his car and dialing Tony's number on his cell phone.

"Hello?" Tony answered.

"Tony? It's Jason."

"Oh hey, what's up bud?"

"Listen you're not gonna believe this, but everything I'm about to tell you is true. We're all in grave danger, and it's because of the DiNAmite."

"What do you mean? Is the Phil thing still freaking you out?"

"Isn't it freaking you out?"

"Yea, actually it is."

"Okay now listen, because this is very important"

Jason said. "You need to stop drinking the DiNAmite. Tell Cloe too. I have some incredible things to tell you guys but you just have to promise me that you'll stop drinking it, okay? And don't tell anyone about this – especially not Phil!"

"Okay man, you got it. I won't drink anymore. I'll tell Cloe too. Oh hey wait a minute, Larry King's on CNN talking about weird things happening to peoples' body parts… kind of like what happened to Phil the other day."

"Really? What's he saying?" Jason asked.

"Hold on a minute."

Jason could hear a faint television sound in the background. Tony turned up the volume.

"Okay, so he's saying all these unexplained things are happening to people," Tony said, "but no one knows the cause of it. And he's got this doctor on and the guy's saying it's just normal genetic diversity and evolution and that kind of thing and there's nothing to be worried about. He thinks the whole thing's being blown way out of proportion. But Jason, the dude's got a tongue like a frog!"

"No way!"

"Yea, wait a minute, hang on" Tony said, listening to more of the conversation. "Okay he's saying that everything's just fine, nothing to be worried about, and we should all be drinking it or else there will be consequences, bad things happening to people, and there's nothing he can do about it."

"Really?"

"Yea, but wait. Okay… he just said that Kenny Graham is a *god* and then Larry just laughed at him and the guy's getting really angry now! Holy shit dude, he just jumped up on the desk!"

Jason could hear a commotion and the guy yelling

at Larry King, *you better fucking drink it!*

"Yea Tony, it's all coming down. Everything they told me is coming true."

"They?"

"I'll explain more to you later."

12 卌

Irascibility

"You know Cynthia, from moment when we first start hitting together, I really knew we make connection" Bossanova said as they practiced on court.

"What do you mean?" Cynthia asked, unsure of where this conversation was heading.

"I mean, I knew we would be great hitting partners, and we can talk everything together. You know... trust friendship loyalty between us... things you don't talk about around other people."

"Yea, I think I know what you mean" Cynthia said. They rallied and Cynthia hit a forehand winner that even Bossanova wasn't able to chase down.

"Oh! Looks like someone has been drinking the DiNAmite!" Bossanova said.

"No, not really" Cynthia replied, which caused Bossanova to frown. "I think it's just that my strokes are getting better, the more I practice."

"Well yes, practice is good of course. But even better is drinking the DiNAmite."

"Oh don't get me wrong, I think it's really good stuff. And well, just look at you! It's obviously doing wonders for your game." Cynthia thought, *and for the size of the horns on your head.*

"You think so? But then why not try more for yourself, if is so good?" Bossanova pressed.

"Oh, I'm sure I will, B. I'll mix it in with my other stuff. I have a pretty rigid routine and diet that I like to stick to for right now, but thanks."

"Hmmm…" was the disappointed reply.

They hit a few more shots, but Bossanova's heart just didn't seem to be into it and Cynthia could tell something was wrong. They took a drink break. It seemed as if she had really hurt Bossanova's feelings by not drinking the DiNAmite. Cynthia figured she would try to get their friendship back on track.

"So B., got any big plans for the holiday weekend coming up?" she asked, hoping to change the subject.

"Yea well holiday weekend, what can I say. Probably same as always."

Left at that, Cynthia wasn't sure what the 'same as always' part actually entailed, but decided not to intrude.

"You know Cynthia, I'm little disappointed" Bossanova finally let on.

"About what?"

"Well about friendship and trust level. You know, I really want you to drink the DiNAmite, because is so good for you. And as my friend I really want you to do as I wish for you. This is so shameful for me…"

"Shameful? B, I said I'd try to work some more of it into my diet and exercise routine eventually. I haven't drank a lot of it, but that's certainly nothing you should feel ashamed about!"

"Yes, I am failing…" Bossanova said, her head falling dejectedly. "My friend does not drink the DiNAmite."

"Okay this is getting a little weird…" Cynthia said. "There's no need for you to get your emotions all wrapped up into whatever kind of sports drink I'm using."

Bossanova's head jerked up unexpectedly and she grew angry. "Is not just 'sports drink'! Is way of life!"

"Okay, okay…" Cynthia said, backing off and hoping to calm her down. "I'm sorry. I didn't realize it was so personal for you." She never realized that Bossanova had such an imbalanced side to her. The more she thought about it, the more she began to feel in danger.

"You know," Cynthia said, "maybe it would be best if we just call it for today. I'm actually really tired and sore anyway from training so hard lately."

"Is not over yet! We have much, much more practice!" Bossanova said, enraged. "But first you must drink the DiNAmite! Here!" she said, pulling out a can, "Drink this!"

"But B, I don't want to drink that right now" Cynthia said calmly but forcefully. "I have my water right here."

"Is full of contaminant, drug, pharmaceutical, plastic leaching all kinds! Is not good for you! Please as friend, drink this, is good for you!" Bossanova insisted.

"Look, I think we'd better just call it quits for today."

"Stupid person! I want to rip your head off! This is whole reason for us playing together, for you to drink the DiNAmite!"

"Really?" Cynthia said. "I thought it was because you were lesbian?"

"Arrggh! I will kill you!" Bossanova shouted, lunging towards Cynthia. Cynthia reacted quickly and ducked out of the way. Bossanova hit the ground hard and lay there for a few seconds, stunned and confused as if trying to shake off a bad hangover.

"What the fuck is wrong with you?" Cynthia asked, grabbing her things and heading for the gate.

Her assailant seemed to have recovered from the spell she was under, or at least realized she'd gone too far.

"I'm so sorry Cynthia! Please come back! I don't know what just happen! Is not my fault!"

⊥⊥ ⊥⊥ ⊥⊥

"I'm not ashamed of it at all" Spigazi said. "As a matter of fact, there's a lot of evidence to suggest the notion that Arizona has been visited in the past by aliens from other worlds."

"Yea, I mean look at you" Jones said. "How could something so ugly come from such beautiful parents as you have. You must have been born from aliens."

"I don't know why you have to be so glib about it."

"Glib? Oooh, now that's a big word for you."

"Not as big as flippant. Or irascible."

"You don't even know what those mean."

"Of course I don't know what they mean" Spigazi said. "But what I'm trying to say is it's almost like a religious experience, to think that we may have been visited by beings from other planets. I mean, just think about the kind of technology they must have. They'd be like gods to us."

"Uh oh, now you're getting all Krakadon on us. Pretty soon you'll be joining a cult and talking about the wonders of genetic manipulation."

"Hey, if it works for them, why not us, right?"

"Because we don't want to look like them" Vaghozi interjected. "They're ugly. We look just fine as we are. We had it right thousands of years ago when we still lived on Arizona, and we still have it right today. We haven't changed at all, except for somewhat larger brains and smaller limbs. It's true, the Krakadon rebels are a bizarre religious cult heavy into genetic manipulation, but let's not forget that they're still Arizonans."

"Why?" Spigazi replied. "They don't claim to be Arizonans. They might as well be dinosaurs. The Earthlings seem to believe them."

"They just haven't seen the error of their ways yet" Vaghozi said. "They'll come around eventually, when the time is right. And speaking of the time being right, we've got to figure out the formula, and soon. Time cannot stand still forever. If Kenny and the Krakadons can go back in time and steal dinosaur DNA then we've got to stay one step ahead of them." Vaghozi shook his head. "I still can't believe they're led by that Special Forces drop-out."

"I still can't believe the Earthlings think they preserved intact dinosaur DNA" Spigazi said.

"You're right, it would never survive 65 million years like that. It's a bullshit story. It could never be mass-produced. But the Earthlings are unaware of our technology, and that is how it must remain. We've already caused enough disruptions to the space-time continuum. We must tread lightly or there could be other unforeseen consequences."

"You mean, besides young Jason Vaghozi?"

13 ㅐㅐㅐ

Enhancements

It was Saturday morning at Denny's and the moon was over my hammy, but in a desperate sort of way. Jason urgently needed to explain everything that had happened to him, everything he had learned during his time with Vaghozi and the alien scientists. He couldn't believe he was even contemplating a discussion about alien scientists, but the freakish twists of reality had dictated events that were stranger than fiction as he sat in the booth, waiting for his friends to show.

He knew he had to act quickly, sharing the secrets with his two closest confidants, and grew afraid of what would happen if he were to be snuffed out before he had a chance to tell them. The DiNAmite peddlers were apparently just the tip of the iceberg: the advance guard of the invading Mongol horde. Yet even the fearless Genghis Khan and all his horsemen were not anywhere near this powerful. He wondered how a simple employee of Murman Outdoor Supply House was expected to turn back the alien tide. He wasn't even a stellar employee. But Vaghozi had mentioned that he only needed to gain access to the facility, not to destroy it, and this thought gave him some comfort. His role in the galactic conspiracy was pretty minimal, when you really boiled it down.

He couldn't believe he just formed a mental sentence with the words *galactic conspiracy* in it. And yet nothing about Phil's tail was make-believe. The people on the news reports with fanged teeth and lashing tongues and scaly skin were not actors either. This was the real deal, as real as it could get. He began to think about how history was calling his name, *Jason Newcastle, savior of the planet*, and recalled something a famous person once said – he thought it was Churchill perhaps: you don't choose your history, history chooses you. It bugged him that he couldn't remember if it really was Churchill who said it or not. It at least sounded plausible that it would be him, but was it really?

"Jason, there you are!" Tony said, arriving with Cloe.

Jason quickly put Churchill and history calling his name away. "Oh, hey guys."

"What time is it?" Tony asked as they sat down.

"9:15" Cloe said.

"Phil's supposed to be here at 9:30, Jason. He said he needs to talk to us about something important."

"Again?" Jason asked.

"I know, last time he had something important he was showing off his new tail, what will it be this time" Tony said.

"Well, that only gives us a few minutes then, and there's a lot I need to tell you guys, so let me get started."

As they sipped on coffee, he began going into the details of his trip to Antarctica, knowing it wasn't just everyone who could brag about their recent visit there.

"So yea, they're this crack team of interplanetary explorers or something – 'explorer-soldiers' is what I think Vaghozi calls them – and they're on a mission to stop these lizard-like alien creatures called 'Krakadons' or something like that from taking over the planet."

"And it's in the DiNAmite?" Tony asked. "The stuff

they're using to turn everybody into them?"

"Yes, that's what they told me" Jason said. "They said they're working on the antidote but it's not ready yet, and in the meantime we need to keep a tight lid on things and not tell anyone else besides us three about it. Oh, and we can't raise any suspicions either. They said just keep acting like everything's normal and just keep ordering the products so Phil and the others won't begin to suspect anything. But just don't actually drink any of it."

"And why do they want us involved?" Cloe asked.

"They said we have the influence necessary to gain access to DiNAmite. Once they have the antidote ready they need us to somehow sneak it in there and do something with it. I'm not clear yet on how all that'll go down, but I may need your guys' help with that."

"You got it bro, whatever you need" Tony said.

"Yea, just let us know" Cloe added.

"Thanks guys. I knew I could count on you" Jason said.

"So who do you think's in on the whole plot? You think Kenny's one of 'em?" Tony asked.

"I don't know, but we'd be safe to assume so. Can't take any chances. Now – Phil – I'm almost certain he's one of 'em."

"Because of the tail?" Tony asked.

"Yea, that'd be the first indication. But also because he's just turned into such a snarly bastard lately, I can't stand him really. Oh come to think of it, I think Vaghozi mentioned something earlier about him already being converted, so it's too late for him."

"Oh, speaking of Phil, here comes Lizard Boy himself" Tony said, pointing out the snarly bastard as he made his way through the front door. Someone accidentally closed the door on his tail and he yelped and snapped angrily in their direction.

"Howdy, boys" he grumbled as he got closer. "And Cloe."

"Hello Phil" Jason said unexcitedly.

"Hey Phil!" Tony said. Cloe piped in cheerily as well, "Hiya, Phil!"

He was uglier than he had ever been before, uglier than Jason could even have imagined he would be. In two days' time he'd gone from sloppy drunk Phil with an emergent tail to pure nasty amphibinoid Phil with tough, leathery looking skin and enlarged nostrils like an alligator. He breathed heavily and seemed to struggle for air most of the time. His movements were jerky and awkward, as if trying to get used to his new and ever-changing body form. His tail had matured into that of a green three foot long salamander and he was no longer wearing shoes, instead walking around barefoot on appendages that were growing fatter and flatter, with sharp toenails protruding a couple of inches from their base. A more hideous sight there could not have been in Denny's on a Saturday morning.

"So great to see you all!" Phil growled pleasantly. "Look, I've been meaning to apologize for my rude behavior the other night at Hooters. I had a little too much in me, I'm afraid. You forgive me, right guys?"

"Oh yes of course Phil, we forgive you" Tony said.

"Really Phil, it was nothing. Don't let it bother you" Jason replied.

"Ahh, you guys are real buds, you know" the half-lizard, half-white guy said. Then he sneezed ferociously and a fine snot mist came shooting out of those huge nostrils, covering the general area.

"Bless… you" Tony said, taken aback by the grotesqueness. Cloe grimaced and Jason just shook his head at what Phil had become.

"I'm really sorry about that guys," Phil said, wiping down his leathery face with a napkin. "So what are we gonna eat? What's good on the menu?"

"Actually Phil, we already ate…" Jason said.

"You did?"

"Yea," Jason said as the other two nodded their heads in agreement. Phil's major etiquette foul had completely dimmed the lights on the moon over my hammy.

"So full…" Tony said, putting his hand to his belly.

"They already took our plates away and everything" Cloe added for artistic effect.

"Yea, we were really just hoping to hear about this important thing you had on your mind" Jason said.

"Oh! Right, right, right…" Phil growled. "Okay, well I'll just give you the condensed version of things."

"Please" Jason said.

"See, you might have been hearing a lot of talk lately," Phil went on, "about whether or not the DiNAmite *may or may not* have anything to do with all of these great changes that are happening to people. You know, like my tail! See, these are what the scientists are now calling 'human enhancements' and they can only be a good thing! And Kenny wants everyone in the organization to know – and that's why I'm telling you guys this – that DiNAmite has *absolutely nothing* to do with any of all this stuff that's been going on. But that even if we *did* have something to do with it, it wouldn't necessarily be a *bad* thing, since all these changes seem to be no more harmless than an improvement upon the entire human race!"

"Kenny said all that?" Tony asked.

"Yes, the man himself put out a big public statement

on it! You see, apparently there's been a lot of suspicious activity going on lately involving DiNAmite; some industrial espionage, Kenny let us know. Now, you boys wouldn't happen to know anything about that, would you?"

"No way, not us" Tony said.

Jason shook his head. "Nothing."

Phil looked at Cloe. She was caught in the headlights. "No, not me" she said quickly.

"Okay, good, that's good to know," Phil said, "because I told Kenny that if I caught *anyone* in my organization who knew *anything* about it, I'd certainly bring it to his attention. You see, whoever is behind all of these human enhancements, well, they're only doing it to make us all better people. We're getting bigger eyes and bigger noses. Bigger teeth even! Some of us can't even *believe* all the positive changes we're seeing in our lives! Don't you agree that it's wonderful?"

"Uh huh… wonderful" Jason replied.

"Oh, Jason, I meant to ask you about something…" Phil said.

"Yes?" Jason's eyes grew larger and his heart began to race.

"I noticed that your PV has gone down slightly – just a little bit from last month's number." He fixed his eyes sternly on Jason. "You're still loving the DiNAmite, aren't you?"

"Oh absolutely! Loving it Phil! Sign me up for more. I could always use a bigger tongue anyway."

Phil laughed heartily and seemed to lighten up. "Now *that's* what I like to hear! I know I won't have to worry about anyone in *my* organization being involved in any of this anti-DiNAmite nonsense!"

14 〄

Cracking the Code

Vaghozi and his team were working diligently in the lab to develop the antidote that would reverse the effects of DiNAmite and bring some sanity and normal looks back to the planet. They'd been working for seven hours straight and Jones needed a break. He began kicking a hacky-sack in the air and singing a ditty that he knew from back home.

> *Glamour ain't everything*
>
> *but baby it's something*
>
> *and fools like me know*
>
> *what you'll never know*

"Yea you are a fool aren't you" Spigazi said.

"Shut up, I'm no fool" Jones replied. "You're the biggest fool on this planet."

"What's a fool?" Spigazi asked.

"Fool, a fool is somebody who doesn't know! And that's not me."

"It's not that you *don't* know" Spigazi said. "It's just that there's no absolute way of knowing that you *do* know."

"Not until we develop the truth serum," Povanti broke in, "but I'm working on that."

"Yes, right after we finish up work on the antidote,"

Vaghozi reminded them, "which we're all working very diligently on right at this very moment."

"Right, right, the antidote" Jones said. "By the way, is there going to be some kind of a reward for coming up with the best name for it?"

"Best name for it?" Vaghozi said, puzzled.

"Yea," Jones said, "you know, like 'Anti-Andro' or 'Get the Lizard Out', you know that kind of thing."

"Oh I don't know, Jones" Vaghozi said. "How about we name it after a song or something."

"How about *The Safety Dance*" Spigazi said. "That's your favorite song, right Jones?"

"No, it isn't, fool! That song's about cocaine!"

"What?"

"Yea, it's about using cocaine! They talk about snorting lines of cocaine pole to pole."

"No they do not…" Spigazi said. "Man, you are dumb!"

"It's true! Anyway it doesn't matter, because my favorite song is *Who's That Girl?*" Jones said. "It's by the Eurythmics."

"I'm not even going there…" he said, walking closer to Povanti, who was peering into a microscope. He had always wanted her. But she had been raised in a science convent, and years of dedication to her studies had turned her into a prude. Her soldierly training had only made matters worse: she not only had the brains, but she also had the body. It was unbearable torture for Spigazi, who on such a dangerous and distant mission was left only with Edison and Jones as completely unsuitable substitutes.

"Whacha looking at, Po?" Spigazi asked in a masculine voice, trying to woo her away from her scholarly pursuits.

"I don't know Spi, but I think I just found your penis in here" she said, completely disregarding her prim and disciplined upbringing.

"Ohh!" the others cried out. She was always ready with the verbal Spigazi repellant.

"No Po, it's not in there, it's right here" he said, grinding his midsection up against her microscope. "That doing anything for you?"

"Yea, it's making me want to vomit."

"Kapow!" Jones said, laughing. "Give it up my man, you ain't never gonna get none of that!"

"Not today at least…" Spigazi said, walking away towards the center of the room, "for I have not the legendary virility of one Colonel Vaghozi."

Vaghozi laughed. "There's probably an operation for that."

"Hey sir," Jones asked Vaghozi, "you think the kid ever caught on to anything about you and him?"

"About what?" Vaghozi asked coyly.

"Oh I don't know," Jones said, "maybe about the fact that you're his real father?"

Vaghozi shook his head. "Nah, I don't think he suspects anything. He was just a twinkle in my eye the night I inter-specially bred with his mother. No way he could remember that. Hell, even *I* don't remember it very well. Had a few too many drinks in me, you see. We'd been surveying the topography around Topeka *all* freakin' day long, before the big battle, so we finally landed in a field somewhere for a little R&R. All I remember was seeing her at this nightclub called the Lazy Eye. Oh, but wasn't she beautiful. I've often thought about visiting with her again.

But you know the rules: no repeat conjugal visits with the Earthlings. One night stands only."

"Yes but that's kind of a dumb rule, isn't it?" Spigazi said. "I mean, the Council doesn't really have a reason for it, do they?"

"Well they say it's to minimize disruptions in the space-time continuum. But also it's for our own protection" Vaghozi replied.

"Yea, everything seems to be for our own protection these days" Spigazi said, frustrated. He looked over at Povanti. "It's not just about chastity locks anymore."

"I got it!" Edison cried out from a corner of the room. "I've unlocked the genetic code for the antidote!"

15 ⊬⊬⊬⊬

Reflections

The three friends leaned against Tony's Jeep at the top of one of the hills just outside of town. It was a briskly cold night and the air was clear. The stars twinkled above; a perfect night for reflecting on one's place on Earth, in the universe, in time. It was, after all, the same stars that Julius Caesar had viewed the night before his death; the same stars that Napoleon had watched on so many sleepless nights as battle awaited him the next morning. And now another major battle on Earth was close to unfolding, for these were the same stars that Vaghozi and his team – as well as the arch-nemesis Krakadons – were observing from somewhere out there.

Tony stared with head up, mouth open, and eyes glued to the stars.

"It really makes you think about our place in this whole big universe, and how small and insignificant we really are."

"We're small," Cloe agreed, "but how do we really know for sure that we're insignificant?"

"Well, I mean maybe insignificant *because* we're so small."

"But there can be nothing greater than the love that human beings have for each other" Cloe said. "I like to think that love is infinite."

"I see it as almost like a giant, infinite computer simulation" Jason said. "Just imagine putting yourself into this infinite plane of existence out there. It could be like that, where we're just a small part of the big picture. But I mean, even if we are insignificant, it doesn't excuse the fact that Cloe wears such bizarre clothing and jewelry."

Cloe giggled. "How else am I supposed to live up to my moniker, most interesting dresser?"

"And eating popcorn for breakfast? Pretty gorky. Explain yourself" Jason said with a joking smile.

"It's like eating corn flakes, only without the sugar!"

"What I don't get guys…" Tony said. "Is why doesn't the media seem to have any clue about what's going on? Why is it that every time you turn on the TV there's some story about how great all the DiNAmite is and how wonderful everyone is becoming with it?"

"It's because everyone who is 'enhanced' seems to love it" Jason said. "No complaints. They talk about having more energy and capabilities. Who wouldn't want that?"

"Well, the Arizonans don't seem to want it" Cloe said.

"Yea, I'm still not sure I'm buying into this whole alien visitation concept just yet" Jason said. "I mean think about it, it would have taken them forever just to get here. The nearest star system is what, seven light years away or so? And who knows if there are any planets around it. The universe is so huge, how did they ever find us? And then how did they reach us so soon?"

"Yea, but you're talking about today's technology" Tony replied. "Who knows what kind of communication technology will exist in 1,000 years from now. There are probably plenty of alien civilizations out there that are thousands of years more advanced than us. Heck, maybe even *millions* of years more advanced than us. They probably create their own universes and travel between dimensions like it's nothing. Who knows, time may mean nothing to them. They could leave one place today and end up thirty light years away tomorrow. It would be just like time standing still for them."

"Can you believe it guys," Cloe said, "that we might be living in a time in history when we first make contact with other intelligent beings? I bet there's so much we could learn from them. And hey who knows, maybe there's a few qualities they admire in us as well!"

╫ ╫ ╫

Kenny called for a meeting with all 1,200 of his direct downlines to discuss the grave situation. The formula had been stolen and nobody so far was having any success in locating the perpetrators.

"No one, huh?" Kenny growled. "Not a damn one of you has any people that knows anything about this? Well, I find that very hard to believe."

Phil wasn't sure whether or not he had useful information, but knew it would be better to err on the safe side. He decided to pipe up before he missed his window of opportunity. Kenny G was known to be capable of doing some very wicked things to people on his bad side. And it had nothing to do with auditory torture.

"Uh, Kenny sir, there is one bit of information I should probably share…" he said, rising to speak.

"Phil, right?" Kenny asked. When you were as successful as Kenny, the view of the faces from the top became a bit blurry.

"Yes sir, it's Phil Mangino. And I have some information about one of my downlines that may or may not be important."

"Well let's hear it then, you're burning daylight son" Kenny replied.

"Okay" Phil continued. "The other morning I met with a few of my downlines at Denny's. I was concerned about these three in particular because their PV hasn't increased lately."

"Okay, and are you kicking it out and knocking 'em in the teeth like you're supposed to be doing?"

"I'm trying sir," Phil replied, "but this one in particular – Jason Newcastle is his name – had a barely detectable level of Pawnium on his person."

"Pawnium? But only the Arizonans use that material!"

"Yes sir, you're correct. Except that it was such a negligible amount that I didn't pursue it."

"Well it's good that you're reporting this, son. I need you to keep a very close eye on that one. If he's been around the Arizonans for long then there's a good chance that he's involved with them."

"Yes sir, he's on my radar screen now. To tell you the truth, he seemed a little too congenial, like he may be hiding something from me. I let him think that he's got me fooled, but I'm on to him. You have my word that he'll be monitored from now on."

"Excellent!" Kenny replied. "Report back to me at regular intervals. I want to know if he even so much as changes his bowel routine, you got me Mangino?"

"Yes sir, I understand."

"Very good then."

"Kenny!" a voice cried out from a distance. It was Kenny's Lab Chief, Fumonda.

"What, Fumonda?"

"Kenny! We've located the Arizonans!"

16 𝍐

Utter Mayhem

Jason made a call on his cell phone from the Starbucks parking lot.

"Tony, I just met with Vaghozi again. He said they were able to formulate an antidote and it would be ready to use within the next 24 hours!"

"They figured it out?"

"They're real close. They're running some tests and things, and then they need us to sneak it inside the DiNAmite plant. It could all be going down tonight."

"But we have the Utter Mayhem Riot tonight! How are we supposed to get out of that?"

"Even better. With Kenny and Phil and everyone else there, that can be our opportunity to get inside the plant somehow. We'll just need to figure out a way to do it."

"Wait a minute," Tony said, "so you think we can get inside DiNAmite *tonight*?"

"It might be our best and only chance. Let's hope Phil will be there."

"He will be."

"Okay, so maybe we can try to butter him up and get him to give us a plant tour. Or maybe Kenny himself would agree to do it."

"How are we gonna do *that*?"

"I don't know. Maybe we can make up something. Maybe tell 'em we just signed up ten new downlines or something. Anything that'll make us stand out more."

"Okay."

"Oh and Tony…"

"Yea bud?"

"Vaghozi gave me some weapons we might need to use… to defend ourselves. I'll bring them tonight."

╫ ╫ ╫

They drove to the Utter Mayhem Riot at Dodge Theatre with uncertainty on their minds. It was by far the biggest MLM event of the year, surpassing even Amway. Thousands would be in attendance, loyally subjecting themselves to a mass indoctrination.

"Utter Mayhem…" Jason said as they drove. "Back home in Topeka it would probably be called *Udder* Mayhem… you know, because of all the cows."

"Yea…" Tony said blankly, seeming distracted. "So Vaghozi gave you some weapons you said?"

"Yea, a pistol and some shock grenades."

"Seriously?"

"Yea, just in case we need them. The pistol's non-lethal. You fire it and it immobilizes your target for an hour or so. I guess the Arizonans don't believe in violence. The shock grenades do the same thing, over a wider area. They're tiny little things. They call them gum balls."

"You have 'em with you?"

"Yea, in my coat. I'm bringing them inside, just in

case things get out of hand. I'm not taking any chances.
You never know."

"Okay, sounds good. I wonder why he didn't give
us more pistols… you know, for Cloe and I?"

They parked and got out of the Jeep. "Not sure,"
Jason said. "But there must be a good reason."

"Probably. You ready to go inside?"

"I'm ready. Let's do it."

"So are we trying to get a plant tour then?" Tony
asked, confirming the plan.

"Yea, let's try that first. But if that doesn't work,
we've got to come up with something else. Maybe just
sneak out unnoticed."

"That'll require some finesse."

"That's my middle name" Jason said.

They put on their name badges and went through
the front entrance. Just inside the hall was the concession
area, where hordes of associates were congregating around
the refreshments, waiting in line to buy the only drink that
was being sold, in three different flavors.

"Looks like we've landed on Tatooie" Jason said as
they observed the curious genetic mutations sprouting from
the heads, arms, and legs of about half of the associates.

"Yea, I think us humans are outnumbered here"
Tony replied.

Unsure of whether or not he was just being
paranoid, Jason felt as if all eyes were on him. He and Tony
found the door to their seating section. As they opened the
door a dude with giant floppy ears bumped into them.

"Oh, I'm terribly sorry" the man said, looking like
the offspring of a gecko and an elf.

"No problem" Jason said as they attempted to make

their way past.

"Ah! You're Jason Newcastle, right? I've heard so much about you!" the elf said.

"You have?"

"Yes! From your upline Phil! Oh, he's sitting right over there if you'd like to sit in his section."

"Okay, great… thanks. You have a real ear for detail. What the heck happened to you?" Jason said.

"What do you mean?"

"Never mind" Jason said, as he and Tony quickly moved on and made their way over to Phil. It was somewhat unsettling that this random mutant in the crowd would be hearing anything at all about him.

"What do you think Phil's been saying about us?" Tony asked.

"I don't know, but it can't be anything good" Jason replied.

"That guy seemed like he liked you though. I mean, at least he wasn't scowling."

"Yea, who knows what they've turned him into though. Weirdest looking reptile I've ever seen."

"Maybe he's an experiment of some kind" Tony suggested.

"Could be. I'm sure his wife's cool with it though. Oh look, there's our buddy."

They approached Phil, and the jolly green asshole welcomed them as if he hadn't seen them in years.

"Jason! Tony! There you guys are! I was hoping you boys would show up!" he said spittingly.

"Wouldn't miss it for the world Phil, you know that" Jason replied chummily.

"Oh, but don't I!" Phil said knowingly.

"How are you, Phil? Sign up anyone new?" Tony asked, as he and Jason found their seats.

"No, not in the last 24 hours. You boys?" Phil asked, flinging more spittle.

"As a matter of fact Phil, my man here has some very, very good news!" Tony said, elbowing Jason and prompting him to spin the plan into action.

"Uh… that's right, Phil! You're probably not gonna believe this, but I signed up *ten new downlines* in the past couple days!"

"Whoa!" Phil was shocked. "Ten new downlines! That's kicking it out, Jason! How on Earth did you do that?"

"Well, I just kept telling myself 'get it down their throats, knock 'em in the teeth', you know, kind of like what you told Tony and I the other day. It really inspired me to try a lot harder."

"How cool is that!" Phil said loudly. "Did you meet some new friends or *what*?"

"No," Jason replied, "I just made better use of the friends I already had. Here, let me get you a towel."

"Well isn't that terrific!" Phil shouted. "Kenny's going to be just thrilled to hear this sensational news!" *Sensational* was like a saliva shower.

"Oh…" Tony interrupted, to facilitate the plan. "Speaking of Kenny… do you think there's any way of arranging a meeting for Jason and I within the next 24 hours or so with him… you know, to celebrate Jason's big achievement? Maybe a ride in his car, like you wanted to do someday? Or… even better… and I know this sounds crazy but it's something we've both always wanted to do… maybe a tour of the plant?" He let it hang out there to see where it would land.

"A plant tour?" Phil said, somewhat taken aback, but quickly warming up to the idea. "Why, that's a great idea, boys! It's the least Kenny could do for ya! This boy's been working hard!" he said, patting Jason on the shoulder with his big sticky appendage. "I'll go talk to him now and see what can be arranged! Hold on for just a minute."

Phil left his seat and tottered towards the stage where Kenny was mingling with the crowd, his gait looking more and more like Godzilla's every day. They watched as he approached Kenny and managed to capture his attention, much too far away and with too much background noise to hear any of the conversation.

"Uh, Kenny sir…" Phil said meekly, out of earshot of his downlines.

"Yes? What is it Phil?"

"Uh, there's someone here I think you should be aware of."

From afar, Jason and Tony could see Phil point them out. From the look on his face, it seemed to pique Kenny's interest.

"That's the one you told me about?"

"Yes sir, that's Jason Newcastle" Phil replied. "He just gave me some line of bullshit about how he just signed up ten new downlines or some shit like that. Get this: now he wants a plant tour!"

"A plant tour? Well ain't that unusual…"

"Well here's the thing, Kenny. I just got word that he was seen getting out of a suspicious looking vehicle earlier today, possibly belonging to the Arizonans. And his Pawnium level is higher than ever tonight."

"Good work, soldier! You won't have to worry about them for long though. We've got a bead on the Arizonans and they'll be taken care of very, very shortly…"

Kenny said. "And as for your little friend over there, I think we need to work a confession out of him tonight. I want you to get him up on stage with me, when the time comes."

"Will do sir" Phil replied and ambled back towards his downlines, displaying two thumbs up and smiling broadly.

"He must have gotten us the plant tour!" Tony said excitedly.

"Yea, maybe" Jason said.

"It's a go, boys!" Phil laughed. "He's extremely interested in having you guys over for a tour and learning more about how you did it!"

"Oh, that's great news!" Jason said, relieved. Incredibly, it seemed as if the plan was actually working.

"Yes, that's wonderful news!" Tony added.

"Yes it certainly is boys, it certainly is…" Phil said, calm and with a satisfied look on his face. "Oh look, I think Kenny is getting ready to speak!"

Sure enough, the ex-special forces soldier had begun shadow boxing as his warm-up song "Eye of the Tiger" was cued up over the loudspeaker. The crowd went fanatical as it appeared the main event was about to get underway.

"Holy shit, here we go!" one man standing next to them shouted, standing up with arms raised and completely immersed in all the excitement.

Kenny leapt to the stage with a knife in his mouth and ran from one end of his elevated platform to the other, a bug-eyed crazy freak with a lethal weapon snug between his teeth. The lobotomized audience was eating it up. Phil was slobbering it up.

"Isn't he *super*!" Phil said.

The hyper-macho performer on stage wasn't ready

to settle down quite yet. He lunged in the air yelling "arrgh!" like a mad man. "Jab, twist, withdraw!" he shouted, making a complete ass of himself… or at least, in the minds of the relatively few unenhanced humans in the crowd. The rest of the zoo seemed to love it. This was what they came for, after all: to be mesmerized by the big tough guy showman Kenny Graham.

"Well alright!" Kenny said, finally beginning to calm down. "I was on fire there for a minute!" he joked, "but I'm better now, I'm better now." He smiled and paced back and forth to the hoots and hollers of the audience.

"You know how you quench the fire? With some of this!" he shouted, holding a can of DiNAmite up in his hand. "This is the magic! This is the stuff right here!" He was sweating profusely and it didn't seem to Jason as if he was in as great a shape as he made himself out to be. A little dancing and some knife lunges and he was spent.

"Alright… well," he said, catching his breath, "have we got one *Hell* of an event planned for you folks tonight, let me tell ya…" Cheers went up from the audience. "Y'all out there are gonna be feeling the power of DiNAmite before this thing's over. Now who wants their PV?!"

A rumble went out from the crowd, everyone shouting in unison "I want my PV! I want my PV!"

"Well we're gonna get to that in a minute folks. But hey, speaking of PV, before we get started I'd like to give a special recognition to one *incredible* associate out there, and I want him to come up on stage and be recognized right now."

Jason looked over at Phil, who was looking back at him and raising his eyebrows in anticipation.

"This is a guy, ladies and gentlemen," Kenny continued, "who just within the past couple of days managed to sign up *ten new downlines*, count 'em, *ten*! Can you *believe* that?" His body twitched like a fire and brimstone southern preacher and he shouted in a gravelly voice, "*That's ten more throats full of DiNAmite!*"

Jason felt a nauseous feeling for the first time as he realized he was going to be under a lot of pressure to pull this thing off, and was beginning to lose confidence in his ability to do what Vaghozi and the Arizonans needed him to do.

"Now think about *that* kind of PV for a moment, will ya folks!" Kenny continued. "So come on down here, Jason Newcastle, you know who you are!" He pointed out into the audience right at them.

Phil prodded him to go up on stage. "Here's your chance, fella!" he said. "Time to shine!"

Jason looked uneasily over at Tony, who wasn't quite sure of what to do next. Neither of them had anticipated this turn of events. The plant tour was one thing: it was per the plan and had the potential to work out beautifully. But Jason wasn't sure of how this could work out quite so well. Overexposure was not desirable at the moment. It brought risks that could not be foreseen. To be recognized was to endanger any plan of sneaking into the facility anonymously. And yet Jason felt as if he had no choice. He knew he needed to play along with whatever happened on stage, and if it led to the plant tour that Phil had assured him Kenny was agreeing to, then he would have the necessary access to sneak the antidote inside and help the Arizonans defeat the alien menace. A flash of insight crossed his mind: it was likely that in his nervousness he was simply being paranoid. Perhaps everything was going as planned after all. He began making his way toward the stage.

"There he is!" Kenny said, laughing and clapping his hands. "Let's give this guy a big round of applause folks! Ten new downlines!"

The audience whistled and cheered, but many of them knew who he was and had their suspicions about him.

Isn't that the one Phil said is with the Arizonans?

Yes, I think that's him.

Jason approached the base of the stage and surprised the crowd by energetically bounding up onto it, taking even Kenny by surprise.

"Whoa, kid's got a lot of energy!" Kenny said. "No wonder he's signed up ten new downlines!"

Jason smiled and walked over to Kenny, extending his hand to shake the CEO's.

"Wow, what a guy, huh folks?" Kenny joked to the audience.

"Kenny, it's a real pleasure to meet you. My name is Jason Newcastle."

"So I've heard, son! So I've heard. And wow! What a strong grip you have, almost broke my bones, haha! But I like that in an associate! That's power!"

"It all comes from drinking the DiNAmite, sir. Gallons of it every day" Jason said.

"But I don't see any enhancements on you yet son... why not?"

It was an admission of the fact that the DiNAmite caused genetic mutations, and yet Jason knew he had to play it cool. He hadn't drunk enough of it to cause any significant changes to his genes, but he also couldn't let on that he had stopped drinking the crap. Keeping the end game of the plant tour in mind, he knew he had to fake it as best as he could.

"Oh, I've got a few enhancements popping up," he said, indicating something hidden underneath his pants that he couldn't really talk about.

"Well alright then, son!" Kenny said. "Maybe there's hope for this one yet, Phil!"

Phil laughed uneasily. It appeared as if Kenny was not entirely convinced that Jason was working with the Arizonans, and was not yet ready to lower the boon on such a hard-working and deferential young man. Kenny seemed to like how important Jason made him feel.

"Alright, well I tell you what son, you seem respectable enough to me, and I think I kinda like ya! You remind me of someone I used to know back in the service. We were friends once, but then he turned to the other side, unfortunately. But that's water under the bridge, so to speak. So I tell you what I'm going to do. I'm going to spare you anymore embarrassment up on this stage. You'll get that plant tour you asked for, you have my word on it."

"Thank you very much sir. I look forward to it."

"Phil, I think you were wrong about this one!" Kenny said, looking out into the crowd right at Phil. "He seems like my kind of *DiNAmite* salesperson! Here, give me your hand, son, let me congratulate you!"

Kenny reached for Jason's hand and held it up high, as if they were presidential running mates. "How about this kid, folks!" he shouted. The crowd was cheering loudly, intensely focused on the drama. But then something fell out of Jason's coat, and he could hear it clink as it hit the floor. He and Kenny both looked down to see what it was.

On the stage, rolling as if in slow motion next to their feet was an orange colored gumball; not the chewy kind but the kind that explode, paralyzing everything within ten feet. Jason saw Kenny's eyes light up in horror: he knew exactly what it was. The two of them dove in opposite directions to get away from the imminent blast.

The gumball went off, leaving Jason and Kenny unscathed. But the crowd began salivating loudly. They now knew for sure that Jason was working with the Arizonans, and Jason knew he was in deep shit. He ran to get off the stage, reaching for his stun gun from out of his coat pocket. A mass of goons ran to block him from his exit. Enhanced human or full-blown alien, Jason didn't care, and he fired indiscriminately in their direction, stunning a wave of them and leaving them frozen in place. Others tried to follow but Jason continued firing in all directions and lobbing gumballs every which way, wreaking mass havoc in the stadium.

"Someone stop that Arizonan!" Kenny yelled from the stage. "Don't let him get away!"

But Jason kept running and gunning, and within seconds he was out the door of the stadium and running into the dark of night. Tony was nowhere to be found and Jason felt awful for leaving his friend behind, but he knew that any attempt to rescue him would be sure suicide. The only thing he could think to do was to somehow blend in to the activities of the public outside and eventually find his way over to the Shack. Vaghozi needed to know that his cover was blown and the Krakadons were on to him. There was no turning back now.

17 𝍷𝍷𝍷𝍷

Going Fishing

"I oughta neutralize you right here and now for being such a pain in my ass!" Kenny scowled at Tony behind closed doors somewhere inside Dodge Theatre. "Fumonda, frisk him. Make sure he's not carrying any weapons. And where's the girl at? Why didn't she come with you?"

"What girl?" Tony wanted to keep Cloe out of this.

"Don't act stupid with me, boy. Do I really look that stupid to you?"

"Well…"

"Ooooh," Fumonda said. "I should slap you so hard for saying that to Kenny."

"You'd like that, wouldn't you."

Kenny was agitated. "You're an awfully brave boy for being in the situation you're in right now."

"He's clean" Fumonda said. "No guns. Pawnium levels are only slightly elevated." He grimaced at Tony. "But he's still a curmudgeon."

"A curmudgeon?" Kenny asked with a twisted up face. "What's that?"

"You know, a curmudgeon. Someone who's grumpy, ill-tempered. Curmudgeon."

"No one uses that word!" Kenny said.

"Sure they do, all the time. I just used it right now."

"You don't even know how to spell it!"

Tony decided to get in on the action. "He doesn't even know what it means, Kenny. A curmudgeon is a crusty old man."

"No, it doesn't have to be an old man!" Fumonda said, ired and defenses up.

"Oh yes it does!" Tony said.

"Look, can we get back on topic here!" Kenny said, annoyed. "We were about to beat some answers out of you. Or I mean, Dr. Fumonda here was about to do that."

Tony laughed.

"What's so funny?"

"He was gonna *slap* me. I guess you could *loosely* call that beating me up" Tony said.

"Oh believe me, I can slap pretty hard, little sassy boy" Fumonda said.

"I bet you can."

"Don't bother, Fumonda. Let's release him. He'll lead us right to the big fish."

"Good idea, sir" Fumonda agreed.

"God, you're such a butt-kisser" Tony said.

"Today's your lucky day…" Kenny began. "We're going to set you free. And what we want you to do is to meet up with your little friends. Gather them all up and bring them all to us over at the DiNAmite plant." He squinted his eyes at Tony, as if issuing him a command through the power of suggestion.

"Sorry, that Jedi mind trick shit only works in Star Wars."

"Oh it works, trust me. It works."

"By the way-" Tony began.

"By the way, why am I normal looking," Kenny interrupted, parroting Tony's thoughts, "and not weird like all the others? Because I'm the face of DiNAmite! I'm the PR guy! There are so many we have yet to convert, we don't want to scare them off. Oh but gradually, don't you worry, we'll convert every last one of you Earthlings."

"Whatever."

"Don't you whatever me, or I won't release you. You're lucky I'm letting you go. We usually do terrible things to those who try to steal our company's secrets."

"Okay, I'm sorry. I won't say it again."

"Very well then. Fumonda, release the bait."

"Fine sir, but I still find his demeanor to be somewhat disquieting" Fumonda said.

Tony cracked a laugh. "Disquieting?"

"Yes, disquieting" Fumonda said huffily. "If you don't know what it means, look it up."

"I know what it means," Tony said, "it's just that you sound like such a dweeb saying it."

"Alright, enough!" Kenny said. "Now go, little fishy! Swim away and catch us the big fish!"

"Oh that 'little fishy' thing reminds me, Kenny" Fumonda said. "I need your advice on something."

"Yea, what?"

"Well, I'm going fishing this weekend, and my friend suggests using something that will anger the other fish so they're more likely to bite. Got any advice on what type of lure to use for that?"

Kenny thought about how best to phrase his response. "Now, how the Hell would I have any advice on that?"

18 ⌗

Shack Attack

Jason ran until he was completely out of breath to get as far away from Dodge Theatre as possible. The Krakadons were sure to follow him, he knew, so it was important to stay in the shadows when possible and try to blend in under the lights when he had to. He desperately looked around for some type of ride to hitch out to Wickenburg some 60 miles north of here, about an hour's drive. His mind raced for a way: *car… truck… taxi… anything*. The police were not an option: they would never believe his story and they would probably arrest him on suspicion of being crazy. There wasn't the luxury of time to spend downtown at the jail, convincing some badge-toting square that he really wasn't making any of this up. *Yes officer, they're aliens. And they're slowly turning us into them by means of a fruity and delicious energy drink. How do I know? Because some other group of aliens told me. There's an inter-galactic war going on, you see.*

Finally he came to a gas station and spied just the sort of hard-up hick he figured might be willing to give him a ride for fifty bucks. He was a scruffy looking young country type, all of about twenty-one, driving a 1980-something Chevy pickup truck and guiding in the last dollar at the pump to an even twenty. He approached cautiously so as not to cause alarm, the experience selling GasMax finally finding some use.

"Uh, excuse me," he said to the young redneck,

"want to make a quick 50 bucks?"

The kid looked surprised by the offer. "Uh… is this one of those kind of truck stops? Sorry buddy, but I'm not really into that."

It dawned on Jason that the question resembled an indecent proposal.

"Oh no, no, no, it's not like that!" Jason said. "I just need a ride out to Wickenburg! I'll pay you for your time, and your gas money. In fact, make it a hundred bucks, to make it worth your while! Please, I just need a little help right now."

The kid thought about it for a couple seconds. "Okay, yea sure. It's a deal then. I'll take you out there. I was heading out that way anyway."

"Oh you are?"

"Yea, I got a cousin who lives there. We're going quad'ing this weekend and I'm staying over at his place."

Jason wished he hadn't just doubled the offer to 100 bucks, but with the fate of the world hanging in the balance, he figured someone from the government would eventually reimburse him at some point, when the smoke had cleared and they were congratulating him on the wonderful job he'd done saving the planet.

"Go ahead, get in and let's roll! The name's Rick" the young country rebel said enthusiastically.

"Jason" he said, hopping in.

As they left the station and turned right onto the main road he could see a couple of familiar faces jogging towards the gas station, unmistakable because of the green horns sticking out of their foreheads: two of the goons he remembered from Dodge Theatre. The Krakadons were hot on his trail. They could probably smell him.

"Step on it, Rick" Jason said.

Rick could tell something wasn't quite right. He saw the two men as they drove past, and Jason slumping in his seat to avoid being detected. He accelerated to put some distance between themselves and the two men, until they were safely out of sight, and merged onto Highway 60 to head towards Wickenburg. Jason felt safely on his way at last.

"Seems like you're running from someone" Rick said, stating the obvious. But put in this way, in such plain-spoken words, it was more shocking than all the gumballs in the world and that exhausting white-knuckle escape from a mob of angry aliens. Speeding down the highway in relative comfort, with the confident hum of the Chevy's engine as a backdrop and some time to reflect, the reality of his fugitive status was beginning to set in. He was a man on the run, and he knew the Krakadons would not rest until they found him.

"You could say that" was Jason's simple reply.

"Ah, don't worry about it, partner. We've all had to run from something or someone at some point in our lives."

The 21-year old kid was steady at the wheel and seemed to possess the wisdom of a man with much more life experience. It was either that or he was used to running from the law. Jason was impressed by his calm demeanor, and thankful that he was there to help him when he needed it the most.

"Yes, I suppose we have" Jason said appreciatively.

Rick turned up the volume on the stereo. It was 'Counting Flowers on the Wall' by Eric Heatherly.

> *Counting flowers on the wall*
>
> *That don't bother me at all*
>
> *Playing solitaire 'til dawn*
>
> *With a deck of 51*

Smoking cigarettes and watching Captain Kangaroo
Now don't tell me I've nothing to do

Jason thought how he would give anything to be doing any one of those activities right about now, with no complaints. But almost an hour of friendly talk and many more songs later: 'A Country Boy Can Survive', 'Private Malone', 'Fishing in the Dark', 'Seminole Wind', 'Traveling Soldier', 'Butterfly', and they arrived at the road in front of the Shack. Jason got out and thanked Rick, handing him his money.

"Nah, don't worry about it partner, this one's on me" he said, waving off Jason's bills. "Keep it for your ride back. And call me if you want to go quad'ing sometime!"

"Okay thanks, I will" Jason replied, and thought that he might just do that at some point, when all this was over. Riding around in the mud on a little motorbike without a care in the world *had* to be more fun than being chased by armed geckos.

"See you later buddy" Rick said, and drove off.

Jason found himself alone in the dark, standing in front of the Shack. It was awfully quiet in there; the lights were on but it appeared that no one was home. Rushing to the front entrance, he found the door wide open. Unfamiliar with typical Arizonan security protocol, he could only hope that this was not an alarming omen, as the idea that the Krakadons had gotten here first – before he had a chance to warn Vaghozi and the others – tormented his mind. Patting his coat pocket to feel the sonic gun still tucked inside, he pulled it out and aimed it at the ready just in case there was trouble. *This is how Captain Kirk must have felt*, the unexpected thought occurred to him as he stepped, attempting not to make any noise. But he was worse off than James T. in at least one way: there was no one beyond the atmosphere ready to whisk away his protons when the situation became unstable. No one was going to be saving his ass in a pinch. In fact, there was not even a single friendly soul to hear him scream. A strange confluence of thoughts occurred to him: if no one could hear him scream, would Einstein have said that he did not really die at all, relative to the non-present observer? Too many discussions about particle physics had complexified the simple riddle of the tree falling in a forest, as he resolved to avoid the topic altogether the next time he became inebriated with friends.

Pushing those distracting thoughts aside, he knew he had to focus on the task at hand. As he carefully stepped around he could hear all of the monitoring instruments at full chatter. And yet there was no talking; just silence, and a mist or some kind of damp smoke filled the air. He quickly scanned for evidence of life or some kind of a struggle, and it didn't take long to find what he was looking for. Turning a corner, there were a couple of bodies on the floor: two of Vaghozi's team. Jason recognized them from Antarctica, Spigazi and Jones. The poor guys appeared to have been neutralized. He gripped his sonic gun tightly and prepared to fire at anything that might attempt to do the same thing to him, moving as quietly as he could past the two bodies. He began to hear what sounded like heavy wheezing from another room: a struggle to breathe. He moved efficiently with weapon drawn to survey for survivors, just like he imagined the Special Forces would do. Peering around the corner he saw Vaghozi still alive, but barely. Immediately, he ran over to his friend.

"Dr. Vaghozi, what happened?"

Vaghozi grimaced in pain as he looked up.

"Starbuck, you're okay…"

"Yes I'm fine. What went on here? Was it the Krakadons?"

"Yes, it was them…" Vaghozi said painfully. "They came here. Found us. Looks like they killed all my team. I'm the only survivor now… if I make it."

"I'm calling an ambulance right now."

"No!" Vaghozi said sternly. "You musn't allow them to think that I survived! They think I'm dead now. But I fooled them. Here…" Vaghozi said, taking out some sort of crystal from his coat. "This is the antidote chip. Starbuck, it is up to you now to get this inside the plant and throw it into the mixing pool."

He handed the chip to Jason. "This chip will react with the DiNAmite to cause a worldwide fumigation" he said, coughing. "It will alter the chemical structure of every single molecule of DiNAmite in existence throughout the entire planet. Nothing can escape from it, not even behind a metal can. It will turn people back into the humans they once were."

"You mean it will reverse all the damage?"

"Yes, that is what will happen. They'll just be normal humans like before they were before… no more Krakadons" Vaghozi wheezed in obvious pain.

"But will that make them go away? Can't they just return with another alien mother ship and a different formula?"

Vaghozi cleared his throat somewhat nervously.

"They're not aliens, Starbuck" he said.

"What? But you said they were."

"I know. But it was an easier explanation than the truth."

"The truth? Then what's the truth?"

"The truth is… that they are humans, just like us."

"Just like us? What do you mean? They don't look like humans. Are you saying you're a human too?"

"Yes, I am. We all are. The Krakadons and the Arizonans both. We're humans from another time and place. We've traveled back here from the distant future. We are what humans will evolve into in thousands of years from now."

Jason could hardly believe what he was hearing. "Time travel? We'll have amazing technologies like time travel and we're going to evolve into *lizards*?"

"Not lizards, Starbuck," Vaghozi wheezed, "but humans will have the power to genetically modify themselves with whatever enhancements they choose, and to precisely control their own evolution."

"Oh my God."

"I would have told you sooner. But I wasn't sure if you were ready for it."

"But… so then why are you guys fighting the Krakadons? Is this some kind of future war?"

"The Krakadons are from what you call the planet Mars, but as I explained before, we have a different name for it now – I mean… in the future. It's called Krakadoa, a name which they gave it after sweeping into power on Mars. They're a very large and powerful force and they've aligned themselves with the rebels here on Arizona. They are a distinct mix of science and religion, bent on achieving genetic perfection for their race by any means necessary and spreading their DNA across the galaxy. They've sent their Special Forces Converter teams out to Arizona in the hopes of spreading their influence, and we've been keeping a close eye on their activities. They believe that by going back in time, they can usher in this genetic perfection at a much earlier day, and induce a return of their God to this planet – a new golden age – and the ability to take over these and other planets in the future. And my team was sent by the Freedom Alliance to stop them."

"Oh my God… this all sounds like the plot from a Terminator movie" Jason said.

"Yea, only way more complicated."

"So why didn't you just stop them yourselves," Jason said, "you know, ATF-style? Why do you need me?"

"Because we're a peaceful people" Vaghozi said, breathing heavily. "We've consistently sought to use non-violent means whenever possible, but those efforts have now failed. Now you're our only hope, Starbuck."

"Can you please stop calling me that?" Jason said. "I never agreed to that name."

"Yes, but listen... there's more I need to tell you."

"More? You mean there's more to this story?"

"Yes... but it will have to wait for another time."

"But what about you? Are you going to make it?" He had never known his father; his mother never talked about him. Growing up, he only imagined how mysterious and brave he must have been. For some strange reason it felt as if his father was dying in his arms right now.

"I don't know, son. It looks like I've been shot a couple times. But if I *do* survive, I'll find that crazy cult leader bastard Kenny G. and I'll annihilate him myself."

"Annihilate?"

"Well, not literally, but because of the hole in space-time we've created, there is a last-resort option: if I can get close enough to him, I have a device that can send the both of us back to Arizona in our own century of time, where hopefully we will catch him and he will face justice. Now, go! You must get the chip inside and throw it into the mix!"

"I will" Jason said sternly, his determination never greater. He took the chip in hand and ran out the door.

"Avenge Meeeeee, Starb-... Jason!" were the last fading words he heard from Vaghozi, as he ran outside into the dark desert night.

19 𝍷𝍷

Sugar Free Pie

Jason left the Shack with the antidote chip in hand, intent on making his way over to the DiNAmite facility undetected and to avenge Vaghozi as he had pledged to do. Now he only wished he had asked four-wheeling Rick to stay a few extra minutes. But the kid and his Chevy were gone, and Jason jogged alone along an empty road in the starlit darkness, with not a house or vehicle in sight.

The city lights of Phoenix served as his compass in the remote desert, as he stopped at the top of a hill to catch his breath. Hesitant to call his friend Tony for fear that the Krakadons were tracing his every move, he decided at last that it was his only option; if the Krakadons found him alone out there he would surely become human road kill. He dialed Tony's number and waited for the connection to come through. It clicked and began ringing.

"Hello, Jason?" Tony said, picking up.

"Tony, you're alright!"

"Yea I'm fine" Tony said. "Are you okay?"

"I'm a little worn out, but I'm okay. What happened back there? Did they do anything to you?"

"Yea, they roughed me up a little," Tony said, "and then they asked me a whole bunch of questions about everything that's been going on, but they didn't get anything out of me. Where are you at?"

It was at that moment – with that particularly direct question – that Jason realized he had become the true runaway fugitive, fully adopting a mentality which made him question Tony's true motives in wanting to know his location. The thought occurred to him… what if the Krakadons were still in the room with him, forcing him to lie, listening to his every conversation and using Tony like chum in the water to capture a bigger fish? He didn't know who he could trust anymore. For all he knew, the aliens had learned to perfectly mimic Tony's voice over the phone. Even talking to his friend, he felt more alone than ever before.

"Tony, what was the name of our favorite fifth grade teacher?"

"Huh? You mean Mrs. Kate?"

"Yea, that's her" he confirmed, feeling more at ease now. Unless the aliens had a way of copying Tony's brain over to a hard drive, there was really no way they could know that little bit of trivia. "Anyway, I'm somewhere close to home."

"You're back in Phoenix already?"

"Almost, but listen Tony. They got the Arizonans."

"What do you mean?"

"They went over there and it looks like they killed them all, every one of them." He was not about to let on that Vaghozi was still alive.

"Oh my God."

"I'm on my way over to DiNAmite right now, and I might need your help."

"Anything bud, of course. I'll be over there – we'll be over there – and we'll meet you there."

"We'll?"

"Oh, Cloe's here. She wants to help too."

"Okay but listen Tony, this is some seriously dangerous shit. The Krakadons aren't playing around here anymore. We're all in danger for our lives."

"Maybe we should tell the police?"

"Yes we probably should," Jason replied, "but then there's no way I'd get into the plant tonight, and the Krakadons would probably just lie and fool everybody. I'm afraid we just have to take matters into our own hands."

"You got it buddy. Are you going to be there soon? Where do you want to meet up at?"

Jason could see the headlights of a slow-moving car coming down the road. At last, a sign of civilization.

"Let's meet in the parking lot at Best Buy and we'll go from there. I thought I was going to need a ride but I see someone coming now. I'll flag them down." He believed it would be safer traveling anonymously for the moment. He would offer up very little information about himself to the driver and just stick to the plan of getting to the Best Buy parking lot to meet Tony and Cloe.

"Okay buddy, be careful. We'll meet you over there soon."

"See you then."

The car was creeping down the road, obviously not in a hurry, and was getting closer now. Jason grasped his gun at his side with his right hand and smiled and waved with his left to catch the driver's attention, hoping he was friendly and clean-cut looking enough not to scare anyone, a lone hitchhiker on a dark desert road somewhere north of Phoenix in the middle of the night. There was nothing scary or unusual about that, he told himself. People do it all the time.

The driver must have noticed him and decided to pull over. The car was in obvious need of brake repairs, squealing as it came to a gradual halt. It was an old Buick. He couldn't make out the driver's face in the headlights so he walked around to the passenger's side to look in. To his amazement it was the same old woman that he had sold his first – and only – can of GasMax to, just a few months before. And here she was, apparently by lucky coincidence, taking the old Buick out for a spin in the sticks. She must have lived nearby, Jason figured, and the thought occurred to him that perhaps Fate was smiling down upon him after all, giving the poor guy a break when he really needed one.

"Well hello there, sonny" the old woman said through her thick glasses. He couldn't be sure that she was legal to drive in her condition, but she was the only horse in town at the moment.

"No kidding!" Jason said. "Do you remember me from a while back?"

The old geezer looked confused, and he worried that he might frighten her if he wasn't careful.

"You remember, the GasMax? I sold you that can! You were very happy about it at the time…"

"Yes, oh yes, I do remember now! My, my, my, what a strange coincidence! Please, get in sonny" she said feebly but quite graciously.

"Oh, thank God you're here! Wow, do I need your help right now."

Jason eagerly got inside and they started to drive. A more perfect cover than this could hardly be found, Jason thought, silently celebrating his good fortune.

"Yes, I remember it" she said again as they accelerated to 20 miles per hour. "And what a delightful product, too. Must have doubled my gas mileage, that one little can did."

"You're kidding me?" Jason said, floored, and wondering if he and Tony had given up the golden goose way too soon.

"Oh yes, I was just tickled by it. Pleased as peaches. Never got a chance to thank you for it though, until now that is" she smiled.

She was the sweetest, most fragile thing, and such a welcome contrast to all of the horrific brutality that had taken place that evening. Jason wished to demonstrate a genuine interest in this kind soul as a way of saying thank you.

"And how are those grandkids of yours?" he asked, recalling the details of his brief encounter with her at the gas station, taken in by the unexpected chance for friendly conversation with someone who, oddly enough, almost felt like family.

"Oh, they're just sprouting up like the alfalfa, you know how fast they grow. It's a good thing they're the only ones getting any older" she winked and smiled, her dry sense of humor gently radiating through.

"I bet, I bet" Jason said, cutting his response short because he realized he'd never told her where he was going. And yet she just kept on driving. They were now on a busier road in town, recognizable to Jason. He found it odd that he never mentioned his destination, and she never asked. It was as if she already knew.

"Oh, I forgot" Jason said. "I never told you where I was going."

"Oh my word, yes you're right. I'm sorry, silly old me!"

"No, no, it's not your fault at all. I'm just so glad you were able to give me a ride in the first place. I'm going over to the-"

"-to the Copper Oven? They have some sugar free

blueberry pie over there that's just DiNAmite!"

Jason looked over at the old woman and could see a long tongue snaking in and out of her mouth as she licked her lips.

"Mmmm…" she said. Then her eyes darted over to Jason and she began laughing loudly and deeply. Much too deeply. It was the laugh of a demon-possessed blue-hair. "You like sugar free pie, sonny?" she asked, disturbingly.

They were at a red light and Jason saw his chance to get out.

"I have to go now."

He opened the door and jumped out onto the street. The old woman's head kicked up in a bout of growling laughter. Her wild frizzy hair and the senility pajamas she was wearing had the effect of making her look like the living dead. Why hadn't he noticed it before? He moved quickly to gain separation, and could hear the old woman's taunts as the Buick limped away.

"I'll say hi to Vaghozi for you… when they finally drop me into the casket! Ah ha ha ha!"

20 ⧾⧾⧾⧾⧾

The Slot Machine

After a harrowing escape from Captain Blue Hair, Jason had had enough surprises for a while. He decided to take a chance and contact Tony again. The DiNAmite plant was only a mile or so from here, but on foot at this late hour, it seemed too risky. There was no telling if the Buick would come back to try to run him down. He called his friend and arranged to meet. Tony arrived with Cloe less than five minutes later.

"Come on, hop in Jason!"

"There you are Tony! Hey Cloe."

"Hey stranger! So I've heard you guys had a big night?"

"You can say that again, and it's only getting started" Jason replied. "I don't know yet how we're gonna sneak in there. We need to figure that part out still."

"Maybe we do it like in the movies, create a diversion or something" Tony suggested.

"Or like in the Wizard of Oz" Cloe said. "You know, knock out a couple of them and take their uniforms?"

"That's a good idea, except they don't have uniforms" Tony answered.

"No, they don't have uniforms…" Jason said, thinking it through, "but they do have delivery trucks.

Maybe we can steal one of them and get inside with it?"

"That's a good idea, you guys" Tony said. "I've seen them come and go a lot actually. Like 24/7. I'm sure we can locate one."

As he spoke, a DiNAmite truck passed them by, going in the opposite direction.

"What are the chances of that..." Jason said.

Tony whipped the Jeep back around and followed the truck as best as he could.

"How far do you think they're going?" Tony asked.

"I don't know" Jason replied. "Maybe try flashing your headlights or something. Get them to pull over."

Tony swerved left and right, flashing his high beams at the truck. It seemed to work and the DiNAmite truck eased over to the side of the road.

"He probably thinks we're the cops" Tony said.

"I'll handle this" Jason said. "You two stay in here just in case this doesn't go well."

"Okay buddy, good luck" Tony said.

Cloe was trembling with fear. She had never been in this much danger before. "He's a brave guy" she said.

Jason approached the truck on the driver's side, hand discreetly on his stun gun, and walked up to the driver's window. The driver was enhanced, looking something like a man-monster who had obviously had his share of the DiNAmite. Jason played it by ear.

"Do you know how fast you were going back there?" he asked, doing his best off-duty patrol officer impersonation.

"Uh..." the manster gaped, "you know, I was never any good at pop quizzes back in school. And come to think of it, I'm still not any good at it. So why don't you just save us all the time and drama and tell me, Mr. Policeman Officer."

Jason couldn't believe the nerve of this genetic misfit, and was thrown off his game plan by the insolent attitude. The driver cocked his head sideways at Jason and looked perplexed.

"You *are* an officer, aren't you?"

"Yes, of course I am" Jason replied as sternly as he could.

"But I don't see any uniform or badge or nothing" he said, continuing to study Jason.

"Well, that's because I'm off-duty." Jason said, stumbling for an answer and beginning to lose his confidence. "But I'm never really *off*-duty. I'm always on the lookout for those who disrespect our nation's laws."

"Nah, I don't think you're an officer" the driver said, then hit upon an idea that caused a fantastically ugly facial expression to emerge, eyes squinting and bulging out at the same time. "As a matter of fact, you look awfully familiar…"

"Well, I don't know why that would be. We've never met before."

"No – I got it!" the beast-man exclaimed. "You look an awful lot like that one they've been looking for! In fact, you mind if I radio in something real quick?"

"As a matter of fact, yes I do mind. You're in violation of Code 43, section 1A" Jason said authoritatively.

But the driver paid no attention, and grabbed his CB radio despite the warning. Jason shook his head and waved to get the driver's attention, to no avail.

"Dispatch, this is Slot Machine. I have something I think you should know" the driver radioed.

"Go ahead Slot Machine" dispatch responded.

But there was no response because Jason blasted Slot Machine with the stun gun, mic still in hand but body completely motionless.

"… Go ahead Slot Machine" dispatch called again, hearing no answer.

"Slot Machine?..."

Jason wasn't sure of what to do next. He pried the mic out of the driver's frozen hand. Whoever was at the other end in dispatch was expecting a response, and might suspect that something was wrong if there wasn't any.

"Uh… this is Slot Machine" Jason began, doing his best imitation of the driver's voice, "I'm going Commando tonight. Over."

"You're what?" dispatch responded.

"Uh… never mind. All clear here. Ten-four over and out."

He motioned to Tony, who got out of the Jeep and came running over.

"Oh man, what do we do with this guy?" Tony said, seeing the creature stuck in position with his hand up to his mouth.

"I don't know, just push him out I guess. We need the truck."

They rolled him out of the driver's seat and left him by the side of the road.

"He'll be fine" Jason said. "They'll find him in the morning. We're all set now, let's go."

21 ⌗

Knock 'em in the Teeth

Security was surprisingly light for the delivery trucks, and a simple garage door-style clicker was sufficient to gain access to the loading docks.

They parked, made a quick plan, and snuck into the facility apparently unnoticed, leaving Cloe behind to guard the vehicle – telling her it was essential – when the actual truth was that they just didn't want to expose her to the risk.

It was already two in the morning. A long and exhausting night was behind Jason, with the threat of even more danger ahead. Yet he soldiered on. They moved quickly, making as little noise as possible. Jason was the only one armed, so Tony followed closely behind, yet at a safe enough distance in case gunplay broke out.

"We're getting closer" Jason whispered. "It should be just around this corner." He said, feeling it instinctively.

"I'm amazed that there's no security, no alarms, nothing!" Tony whispered back as they scampered down a long hallway.

And then the alarm system went off, echoing loudly in the non-acoustically engineered hallways. Bright strobe lights flashed their emergency warning, and the seductively pleasing female voice announced over the loudspeaker, "Sector 30… Sector 30… Sector 30" as if inviting you there to meet for drinks and a little late-night rendezvous.

They knew they were in big trouble. A feeling went through Tony's mind and he was taken back many years – to grade school – to an incident that he had forgotten about, until now. There was a time in the third grade, in Miss Benson's class, when each student brought in some kind of candy or baked good, to celebrate something or other that the class had supposedly accomplished. He was so hungry that day, and so overcome by the sight of all those goodies, that he pulled the school's fire alarm and hid in the bathroom until everyone else had run outside. Then, when he was sure the coast was clear, he snuck back into the classroom and had his way with all those wonderful cakes and pies and pieces of fudge, quickly devouring handfuls of them as if in a timed eating contest. It didn't take long for school officials to pin him down as the culprit: the fat kid gone missing during role call coinciding with the sensational devastation of the cupcakes and pudding. He was grounded for six weeks and nearly expelled from school for it, but it was a priceless memory that he wouldn't have traded for anything. And now at this moment, it felt as if his secret reward was just around the corner again, all for the taking.

"Sector 30… Sector 30." The two friends were sure the Krakadons would rush reinforcements over to the area – or whatever they still had available at this late hour – and yet no one came to stop them.

"Just seconds away now, I think" Jason said.

As they rounded the corner they came upon Sector 30 in all its glory: a walkway with lighted control panel on a narrow pathway over a giant vat of liquid that could only have been the source of the DiNAmite formula. This was it. They had arrived where they needed to be, to throw the chip into the giant foul cesspool of genetic material.

"There it is!" Tony shouted. "Throw it in, Jason!"

Jason reached for the chip from inside of his coat pocket and held it firmly in his hand for a brief moment – a glint of light shining off of it – then hurled it as hard as he could towards the vat of DiNAmite. The chip arched through the air in slow motion, spinning like a wheel towards its intended target, and nearly making it there before being swatted away by a tennis racquet.

It was Bossanova, Cynthia's beastly tennis partner, fully enhanced and apparently serving as guard dog to the DiNAmite formula.

"Such a weak toss... like dainty princess girl!" she said to Jason. The swatted-away antidote chip landed at his feet and he picked it up. She taunted him again. "If only you drank more of the DiNAmite, little boy, perhaps throw would be much stronger."

"Yea, and I'd be a whole lot uglier too" Jason said.

Bossanova just laughed. "What you see is future woman, little boy."

"Thank God we're not living long enough to see it" Jason said.

Tony laughed. "Good one Jason!"

"No..." Bossanova agreed. "Not living long enough, of that I am certain. Here," she said, throwing a racquet to each of them, "since you love tennis game so much and won't leave Cynthia alone, let us decide by game-set-match of death."

"Leave Cynthia alone?" Jason asked, confused, catching one of the racquets.

"I always suspected you two had a lesbian thing going on" Tony said, getting in a dig of his own.

"Tony!" Jason cried in disbelief. "Cynthia's not a lesbian!"

"Okay, sorry Jason, I was just trying to piss off She-Man over there" he said, pointing with the other tossed racquet.

"I don't think that takes much" Jason replied.

"No, she is not lesbian, she make very clear to me" Bossanova confirmed.

Jason busted out laughing.

"What is so funny, stupid little boy?" she growled at Jason.

"Oh nothing."

"Good, then where was I? Oh yes, game-set-match of death. You each have racquet. Now let's... how do you say... *get it on*!"

She took a couple of powerful steps and somersaulted through the air, grunting loudly and landing right between Jason and Tony. Swiveling her tennis racquet through the air like a samurai fighter, her nostrils were bigger than ever as she egged them on to fight. First she lunged at Tony.

"Ahh!" Tony said frightingly in disbelief at what was happening, blocking Bossanova's swings with his racquet and making a hasty retreat backwards.

Jason saw that his friend was in desperate trouble and yelled out with a warrior cry that shocked even himself as he charged at Bossanova. The beast swung around to parry his thrust and they matched swings tit for tat in a fierce battle that was like a bad commercial for Prince and Wilson racquets.

"Why are you here, anyway?" Jason asked between swings.

Bossanova growled and shrieked as she struck powerful blow after blow that Jason could barely fend off. She was beginning to sound like a werewolf as her testosterone level peaked.

"Because I work here!" she growled. "In fact I am Employee of Month!"

And with a mighty swing she knocked Jason's racquet out of his hands. Pinning him down on the ground, she raised her racquet to deliver the fatal blow, but was whacked across the back by Tony, confusing her momentarily. She became irritated when she realized what had happened.

"Come here, little fat boy!" she shrieked, giving chase to Tony and running him down. Tony began to cry as the monster jumped on top of him and began to punch him repeatedly. Jason got up from the floor and recovered his racquet. Running over to Bossanova, she could not hear his footsteps as he raised the racquet into the air.

"Game, set, and… MATCH!" he yelled, swinging the racquet across the back of the beast's head and knocking her out cold. "No one hits my friend like that!" he yelled at the unconscious Bossanova lying on the floor.

"Good shot, Jason! A lot of topspin on that one. Thanks for saving me buddy!"

"You're welcome. And thanks for saving me too."

A voice came out of the shadows. "Well done!" it laughed wickedly.

It was a familiar voice. Jason and Tony both knew who it was before they could even see Kenny.

"Well done, indeed! But contrary to your mutual flatteries, it is not in fact enough to actually *save* you. Although I must say, I am impressed by how much you two *do* seem to get around. Or was it the Jedi mind trick that brought you both here?"

Tony had called bullshit on Kenny's hypnotic twitching at the time of his interrogation, but now had to wonder if the gimmick had worked after all.

"Why, Jason," Kenny continued, "it seems like only a few hours ago that we were all congratulating you on your marvelous achievement! Ten new downlines, how about that!" He paced back and forth for good measure as he spoke. "Only, as it turned out, it was all just lies and you were working for the Arizonans! Hmmm... and even *I* was beginning to believe you, before you stirred up the convention with your little heroic display of bravery. Phil was right, we should have neutralized the both of you like we did your friends Vaghozi and his pathetic crew. Did you know he was in charge of the Special Forces school? Elite soldier-scientists, my ass! But then, I always knew from my days back in the so-called Freedom Alliance that that old fool wasn't all he was cracked up to be."

Jason was steel-nerved and leveled a strong spoken resolve. "You killed those innocent people for no good reason, except your own nutty and twisted religious beliefs, and you're going to pay for what you've done!"

"Jason, what are you talking about?" Tony asked.

"They're not dinosaurs or aliens, Tony, they're just men. Just obsequious, selfish, sad, delusional men, no different than today's man or the cave men of the last Ice Age. Except that these men have traveled back in time. Kenny and his fellow DiNAmite thugs are here from the future, and they're under the mistaken impression that they can usher in their God's return just as soon as we all become genetically perfect like *them*."

Kenny clapped his hands in mock congratulations. "Amazing! Okay, I'll play along with all this delusional nonsense... someone has earned their gold star for the day!"

"It's all true, admit it" Jason said.

"Oh sure, sure! Yes, it's all so very true! Well, I mean take out all the whiny editorializing and *then* it's true. But make no mistake about it, my dear little overachiever. If our prophet Krakadoa has told us it is to be so, then so it is to be."

"Your prophet's full of shit" Jason said angrily.

"You guys haven't evolved at all. Oh sure, you look different, but one thing I also learned in school is that looks aren't everything."

Kenny grimaced. "Ouch, that hurts."

"It should" Jason said. "I'm really pissed about how much you and your cronies have been contaminating our gene pool. And now I'm going to throw this antidote chip right into that toxic soup and ruin all your wonderful plans" he said, raising the crystal in his right hand. "Sorry Kenny, but the Second Coming's been canceled!"

"Wait!" Kenny said, frantically waving off the idea. "You don't have to do that! You know, there are plenty of other options here for us Jason… like, for example, perhaps a diet version of our popular drink would allay your concerns? I mean, at least it would be healthier?"

Jason laughed in disbelief. "Are you serious?" He looked over at Tony. "It's funny Tony, but for supposedly being such a Special Forces soldier and everything, he sure does sound a lot like a giant wuss , now that the tables have turned."

"Yea, maybe Special Forces in the Salvation Army!" Tony said.

"Oh, the Special Forces bit?" Kenny interjected. "Okay, okay, you're right. It was all made up. I never spent a day of my life there. Okay well that's not quite true either. Confession time: I was there for a while. But I refused to eat snakes. I never forgave Vaghozi for kicking me out of his program just for that stupid little reason. Oh sure, I spent some time in the Freedom Alliance afterwards, when I was young and misguided. So I've just been putting on a good show, you know, for morale! Multi-Level Marketing is not easy, you have to have someone to look up to! Someone you can trust with every dollar you have. Someone who would never lie to you! But Special Forces? It's all just for show. It's all bullshit. I'm not part of anything like that."

"Obviously…" Tony said.

"That sure was a long way to go to tell us you're a fraud" Jason said.

"And what about all those cars you supposedly have?" Tony asked. "What are you driving on this day of the week? A Lamborghini? A Ferrari?"

"Huh?" Kenny asked. "Oh! Oh, the cars thing, right! Yea, that was all made up too. I don't drive a new car everyday of the week. I lease a sensible, fuel-efficient sub-compact."

"Oh my God…" Tony said.

"Now seriously boys," Kenny continued, "let's just try to be reasonable and let's just put that chip down. It won't do *you* or any one of us here any good, and it can only lead to bad things."

"Don't listen to this fake asshole" Tony said. "Throw it in, Jason!"

Kenny realized his deception wasn't working and became angry. "You know what, I've heard just about enough out of you! I am *not* a fake asshole, I'm a real one!" He drew a gun and blasted Tony with it. Tony stood frozen in place.

Jason was horrified. "Tony?" he said. But his friend didn't move.

"Oh, don't worry," Kenny said, "he only *looks* dead. It's just a stun gun." He displayed the piece. "Seems to be a lot of that going around tonight, eh Jason?"

"You're never gonna get away with this" Jason said angrily.

Kenny mocked his words. "*'You're never gonna get away with this'*" he said, laughing. "Isn't that what they all say, my little hero? And yet, who is going to stop me now? The news media is clueless. My underlings all worship me like I'm some kind of a fucking *god*!" He was fond of making the comparison.

"But you're nothing of the sort" Jason replied. "In fact, I think your 'enhancements' suck!"

"Oh, but that's not what everyone thinks, oh no no no. Remember Miss Bedroom Eyes?" Kenny asked giddily. "Just ask her what *she* thinks of my enhancements."

"Oh my God…"

"Yes, that's what she said, too."

"You're a sick bastard."

"Oh but on the contrary, there's nothing at all sick about me. In fact, I'm very healthy! Because I drink what you refuse to drink. And look where it's gotten *me*, and look where it's gotten *you*."

He walked around a few steps, savoring his moment of triumph and the fact that he had everyone right where he wanted them. Instead of talking with his hands he was waving his gun around.

"Your pathetic Arizonan friends have all failed to stop me. And *you're* obviously in no position to be making any demands. And so now I'm free to pursue my ambition of making the human race genetically pure at long last and expediting the arrival of Krakadoa to this planet, to wipe the slate clean and begin anew! I shall go down in history as the greatest contributor to mankind's progress *ever*!" he said dramatically.

"No…" Jason said, as if to reject his statement, while discreetly looking for cover. "You won't be going down in any history books. Because there's just one little thing you've forgotten about."

Kenny was confident there was nothing he had forgotten. "Oh? And what's that?"

Jason held the chip in front of him. "I have the

chip."

But it didn't seem to bother Kenny. "Oh yea? Well I have the gun," he said dismissively, "and it's pointed right at you. Now hand over that stupid little chip, Mr. Ten New Downlines, if you know what's good for you. The Arizonans made it, after all, so it's probably botched anyway."

"Oh it works…" Jason said.

"Yea? And how would you know?"

"Hey guys, where are you?" Cloe said as she rounded the corner, momentarily distracting Kenny. Jason saw his opportunity and seized it, heaving the chip as hard as he could. Kenny aimed the gun at Cloe and fired. She froze in place next to Tony, motionless as the antidote chip hurtled through the air towards the vat of DiNAmite. Only inches from splashing, a ten-foot long tongue lashed out and stole it away.

It was Kenny's tongue, enhanced like a frog snatching a fly. He pulled the chip from his sticky lips and held it in his hand.

"Didn't see that coming, did you?" he laughed ferociously. Jason was speechless and couldn't believe what had just happened. The chip was now in Kenny's hands and there was nothing he could do about it. There was no way to stop him. His friends were frozen and a gun was pointed right at him. All hope was lost.

Kenny motioned with his gun. "Anymore of your friends hiding back there? Tell 'em to come out!"

Jason was silent and refused to say anything. His fate was sealed. Kenny was sadistically elated.

"You know, I'm *really* going to enjoy watching you and your two friends here, as we put you through our accelerated enhancement program, making you absolutely genetically *perfect* in under an hour! Oh, you'll be one of us in no time, eager to share the good news about DiNAmite! Kickin' 'em out and knockin' 'em in the teeth!"

The timing could not have been more à propos. Jason could see Vaghozi swing through the air as if on a vine from above, flying straight towards Kenny.

"Like this!?" the doctor said as his feet introduced themselves to Kenny's face at 30 miles an hour. The impact was so great it knocked Kenny down and sent the antidote chip flying through the air, landing only yards from where Jason stood. He scrambled to get the chip as a fight ensued overhead.

"Colonel Vaghozi! You were supposed to be dead, old man!"

"Guess I didn't get the memo!"

"I should have finished you off back in Topeka when I had the chance!"

"Yes, failure seems to be the only thing you're good at! Now it's payback time for what you did to my team!"

Kenny lunged for the gun that had been knocked out of his hand. "I got your payback right here old man!" he said, turning to fire at Vaghozi. But the Special Forces scientist back-flipped out of the way and the shots missed. Kenny's weapon jammed.

"Jason, throw in the chip!" Vaghozi shouted as he gained close quarters with his nemesis, struggling for control of the weapon. "How dare you jump ship and join DiNAmite!"

"What was I supposed to do when you decided to change the TSS formula," Kenny gritted as he and Vaghozi locked arms in a stalemated test of strength, "sit there and watch New Coke happen all over again? It's *free*, for Christ's sake!"

"Free… does not mean… *cheap*!"

Jason grabbed the antidote and threw it as hard as he could. This time it found its mark and splashed into the DiNAmite. A green cloud erupted from the liquid vat and quickly engulfed the two combatants overhead. The sounds of fighting subsided as the two of them disappeared into the mist.

And then there was no sound at all; just silence and an expanding green haze that soon permeated the entire room. Jason stood by his two friends until the effects of the stun gun wore off, but Kenny and Vaghozi were nowhere to be found.

22 卌

Superstar

It was Monday morning and Jason was back at MOSH, an incredible couple of days now behind him. Unsure of how to respond to the age-old query *how was your weekend*, he thought of the good people who had lost their lives and the sacrifices they had made to save the planet from an insidious danger that had threatened to destroy all of humanity.

He reached his cubicle and turned on the computer. Alice was already jabbering on the phone on the other side of the wall; something about the restaurant where her husband worked being shut down for numerous code violations. *Yes, can you believe that? Couple of real jerks. Name was Mickey or Monty or Moby or something like that. And they acted like they were proud of how many violations they could find on the place.* He wondered if one of the violations was for ant infestation, caused by M&Ms left out in the open. If they could only inspect this place, he thought, not yet ready to sit down in his chair.

Glancing across the tops of the cubicles he could see Cynthia walking into the break room, and decided that he would walk right over there and ask her out. After what he had been through, he felt there was no longer anything he was afraid of anymore.

"Hi Cynthia" he said cheerily, yet trying to appear as casual as he could.

"Oh, hey Jason. How are you?" she replied, mercifully not inquiring about his weekend, perhaps because it really didn't interest her all that much.

"Not bad for a Monday morning, I suppose. Hey, did you get to play any tennis this weekend?"

"No" she answered. "Bossanova was MIA on Saturday. I finally heard back from her on Sunday, but she said she had a real bad headache."

"Oh my gosh, that's awful" Jason said. "Maybe she was upset about the whole incident with the DiNAmite plant shutting down."

"Yea, I saw that on the news" Cynthia said. "What happened with that?"

Jason shrugged his shoulders. "No idea. But hey, look at the bright side. At least now maybe she'll stop pestering you about drinking that stuff."

"Yea, she can be pretty persistent sometimes."

"Tell me about it" Jason said.

Cynthia was curious. "And how would you know?"

"Oh… she and I swung racquets a bit this weekend."

"You played tennis with her?"

"You could say that."

"Hmm, I wouldn't have expected *that* out of her."

"Yea, it surprised me as well."

He knew he had to put the conversation back on track and strike while the iron was still hot, lest his moment of courage pass him by.

"Hey listen Cynthia, I was wondering if you'd like to hang out together sometime… when you're not busy that is. You know, maybe go out for a bite to eat, or to a movie or something."

She hadn't yet said anything, but Jason could tell by the minute twitchings of her facial muscles that the answer would be a resounding *no*.

"Umm... well, I'm usually pretty busy all the time, is the thing..."

"All the time?" Jason said. "You mean like, you never take a break, ever?"

"Yea it's really weird, I know."

Jason decided to put it all out there. "I'm just not your type, am I? I mean let's face it, I really like you, but you don't feel the same way *at all* about me."

"It's not that I don't like you, Jason..." she said. "It's just that... well, I don't want to limit myself to just the people here at work. I mean, just to give you an example of the league I play in, I just got an offer to go out on a date with the guy who does the Kool-Aid commercials. You know, the guy who plays the Kool-Aid man and busts through the brick wall and says *Oh Yea* to everybody? He asked me out. And honestly that's the kind of superstar I'm looking for. You know, someone who can change the world." She laughed. "It sounds like such a cliché, I know, but..."

"No, I hear ya, I hear ya" Jason said, raising his hands to indicate that he was backing off, disappointed that he apparently wasn't good enough, but relieved that he had at least had the courage to ask her. "I certainly don't want to be as persistent as Bossanova about it. Thanks for your honesty though."

Cynthia flashed her well-practiced smile.

"I knew you'd understand" she said, and walked away.

Tony had been listening to the conversation from

outside the break room. He approached his friend with a consoling, "She's a tough one, huh."

"Yes she is" Jason replied. "But I think that was pretty much the end of the line, as far as she and I go. She made that pretty clear."

"If you'd only saved the world."

"Hmm, yea" Jason scoffed, "or done some commercials."

"Hey, listen" Tony said. "Cloe and I are gonna hit up a movie tonight. You're more than welcomed to join us if you'd like."

Jason was appreciative but not in the right frame of mind. "Thanks Tony, but I think I'll just chill out on my own tonight. I've got a lot on my mind and just need some time to think things through."

"Yea, I understand" Tony answered. "It's been a really weird week for all of us. Phil called me last night. He wants to make amends. Says he's real sorry about everything. He hasn't changed much though: he called from you-know-where. Said he could probably hook you up with Bedroom Eyes if you wanted."

"Uh… I'd have to say thanks but no thanks, after what I found out this weekend about her."

"Really? What did you find out?"

"Well you were there. Oh, but maybe you weren't able to hear it. Kenny mentioned something about her while you and Cloe were still frozen. I'll tell you later. But I think I'm gonna avoid Phil for a while, at least. The whole ratting-us-out thing is gonna take some time for me to get over."

"I hear ya."

23 〣

Irreversible

Jason sat at home alone that night. He had saved the planet and there was not much else to do now besides watch TV. Surfing across the channels looking for something interesting, he found handbags, magical detergents, reality shows featuring various kinds of drama, and homes you could pick up for $300. Tony had probably already given them his credit card number.

He changed the channel again and there was live coverage of the incident at DiNAmite. The news van was parked at the front entrance, its crew speaking with a familiar-looking man wearing blue overalls. Jason couldn't believe his eyes. He knew that face. It was Spigazi from Dr. Vaghozi's elite team of time traveling soldier-scientists, except that he wasn't dead, he was giving an interview for Action Four News.

"Well there's certainly been a lot of strange goings-on happening here lately at DiNAmite, wouldn't you agree?" the voluptuous news sleuth asked.

"Yes, there certainly has been" Spigazi answered. "And I think it's safe to say that with all that's been happening here lately, it's clearly not safe to drink DiNAmite anymore, which is why I'm here today to promote a brand new alternative, *Arizona Free*." He raised a silver can with bold blue lettering.

"Arizona Free?" the reporter asked. "Quite an unusual name for an energy drink."

"Well, that's because it's quite an unusual product."

"Can you tell us more about it?" she asked, obviously being paid under the table for the interview.

"Sure I can. You see, *Arizona Free* is a rebranding of our popular energy drink *Time Stand Still*, or TSS as you may know it. It has zero calories, and yet retains all of the wholesome goodness you'd expect from us, such as being sourced from the Hassayampa River. It's good for your body *and* the planet. And just like our company motto, we're breaking the laws of physics. How you ask? Well, the laws of physics just won't allow for the average person to travel through time. But *Arizona Free* skirts around this so-called law. Now, it doesn't actually give you more time, oh no no no. Instead what it does is that helps you to do more with the time you already *have*. You see, it's as if by drinking this product, you may enter into any number of parallel, alternative universes, where anything is possible. We can't guarantee the outcome. But we can guarantee you this: it will be unexpected." He turned to look directly into the camera. "Our CEO Dr. Vaghozi wants you to know that it's because of loyal fans out there like Jason Newcastle that Arizona is truly and actually *free* now."

The loyal fan sat frozen with his mouth open looking at the TV set, not from any stun gun, but because he simply couldn't believe what he was seeing.

"See what I mean?" Spigazi said. "Alternative universes. You weren't expecting that, were you?"

He thought through what must have happened to him: how the barista had spiked his drink at Starbucks just before he met Vaghozi, and he reminded himself to avoid that vast frozen ice sheet of a continent in the future, and baristas named Povanti. He recalled Phil one night at Hooters saying *it'll trip you out*. That bastard had been right about one thing after all.

⊥⊥ ⊥⊥ ⊥⊥

"Those damn Arizonans!" Kenny said as he transferred clothes from the washer to the dryer. "They blew up the formula *again*! Turned my clothes all green and sooty!"

"Here, try one of these" Fumonda said, handing him a dryer sheet.

"What's this for?"

"It'll make your clothes come out smelling all fresh and clean. Softer too."

Kenny looked at the sheet for a second before dismissively throwing it into the dryer. "*Next* time, we're changing our company logo to something a little more cute and cuddly than *lizards.*"

He noticed the bottle of fabric softener. "Like this cute cuddle bear here. *Nobody* fucks with a cuddle bear! They're too cute and loveable. And anyway if they do, you just rip their fucking heads off!"

"Good idea, boss" Fumonda said.

"And I thought of another name we could use for our conversion fluid instead of DiNAmite. What do you think of this: *Phoenix Energy.* I even thought of our little tagline too. How does this sound: *Phoenix Energy: Get Up Off Your Ashes.*"

"That's another great idea, boss… or, or maybe something like this: *Zombie Energy: Rise from the Dead*?"

Kenny looked at Fumonda with a scrunched up face. "That's the stupidest idea I ever heard of!"

"You're right boss."

"And besides, it's already taken."

"Okay, okay, I got another one then" Fumonda said. "How about this: *Big Bang Energy: Blow One Up*."

"Blow one up? What is it, an energy drink or an inflatable doll? No, no, I think we need something a little more definitive than that" Kenny said, pacing the floor. "Can you believe Vaghozi had them all believing that we're actually *aliens* from the *future*? I tell you, the lows these people will sink to. But all is fair in love and energy drink wars, I suppose."

"Well, that's the lying, unethical TSS crowd for ya" Fumonda said. "And don't forget the peyote they've been putting in there."

"Oh, yes, the peyote" Kenny said. "They'll get caught one day for that, mark my words. If the FDA can bust our chops over some fucking *roaches*, you'd better believe they'll come after them for that. It's probably why they changed the formula to that 'Arizona Free' crap. Free of reality-altering peyote!"

"Probably, boss."

Kenny embarked upon on an optimistic train of thought. "Anyway, the damage is not irreversible, Schmeckles. We can still fix this."

But Fumonda was confused. "You mean… it's *reversible*, right?"

"Yea, that's what I said, it's not irreversible. That means you can reverse it."

Fumonda pointed into the air as if mentally diagramming a sentence structure, trying to figure out the correct grammar.

Kenny yanked the laundry basket away in frustration. "Give me that!"

www.ingramcontent.com/pod-product-compliance
Lightning Source LLC
Chambersburg PA
CBHW020130180626
46810CB00004B/1479